Shifting Waters

Secrets of Mackinac Island

Katie Winters

Chapter One

Twenty-five Years Ago

That February on Mackinac Island, thick clouds cloaked islanders with a shimmering blanket of snow. Twenty-two-year-old Cindy Swartz reveled in it, flying down the hill on their sled near Fort Mackinac alongside her two younger siblings, Tracey and Alex. She cooked warm and nourishing soups and chilis for her man, the freight-worker Jeremy Miller. Her high school sweetheart, the love of her life, and the man she couldn't wait to marry someday.

That winter, the temperature had been temperamental, rising to thirty-three at some points before dropping violently back to below zero. Despite inconsistent weather, Mackinac Island refused to give up on its iconic "Ice Bridge to Mackinac Island Race" where islanders and tourists alike drove their snowmobiles across the ice from St. Ignace to Mackinac Island, where they joined a Winter Festival of eclectic music, hot cider, warm food, and plenty of partying.

On the morning of the Ice Bridge to Mackinac Island Race,

Cindy awoke to a gray light across Jeremy's comforter, which she'd unconsciously rolled herself up in throughout the early morning. A note on the bedside table read:

See you at the finish line. XOXO.

Cindy's heart leaped with excitement. She brought the little note to her lips, kissing it gently, and returned it to the table. Just as he always did for his career on the freight liner, Jeremy had had to wake up around four that morning, tiptoe around the apartment, take the world's quietest shower, then rush out into the chilly night, all before she'd bothered to wake. The most incredible feat of all, to Cindy, was that he managed to stay up just as late as she did, drinking coffee around seven at night to make sure they didn't lose a moment together. *"When we get to talking, we just can't shut up,"* Cindy had explained to her sister once, her heart brimming with pride.

One thing she'd always told herself was: Don't get into a marriage like your parents. Dean and Mandy Swartz weren't like two puzzle pieces. They were oil and water, both upholding the institution of marriage like a beacon. *And for what?* Cindy wondered. Her brother Alex resisted the idea that their parents weren't right for one another, but Cindy thought you had to be insane not to see it. Their unhappiness was written clear across their faces.

Cindy limped out of bed, showered beneath a scalding, torturous stream, then wrapped up in the comforter again to dial Tracey, who still lived full-time at their parents' place on Pontiac Trail Head. Only the richest islanders lived up there on that glorious hilltop, with a perfect view of the Straits of Mackinac and the Mackinac Bridge. Dean had moved the family there after his career had taken off on the island. A once lowly production assistant for films and theater productions suddenly owned half the hotels and bed and breakfasts on the island— with some ownership in Mackinaw City, as well.

Almost overnight, the Swartz family became a name synonymous with Mackinac Island wealth.

But Cindy wasn't sure she wanted anything to do with it.

"Hello?" Mandy Swartz answered, bright and chipper as ever. All mothers across the earth seemed to wake up by five.

"Good morning, Mama!"

"Hi, sweetie. You sound happy. Today's the big race, isn't it? Jeremy is already headed to St. Ignace?"

"That's right. He had his snowmobile shipped over there a few days ago."

"How exciting," Mandy replied dreamily. "Your sister's just gotten out of the shower. Says she plans to join you."

Suddenly, there came the chaotic sound of Tracey rushing toward the phone to grab it away.

"Hey!" Mandy cried playfully.

"There you are!" This was Cindy's "kid-sister," Tracey. Tracey was only one year younger than Cindy was, but there was a youthful optimism to her, something Cindy had never managed to crack. You had the sense that Tracey would find a way to never have to grow up, like a modern-day Peter Pan (with better fashion). (And really, Tracey had better fashion than anyone Cindy knew.)

"What's our plan today?" Cindy asked. "You want to come over for breakfast before the race? Tara's coming, too." Tara was Cindy's best friend since childhood and essentially part of the family, a third sister.

About thirty minutes later, both Tara and Tracey stomped their boots of snow at the front door of Jeremy's little apartment in downtown Mackinac, two shops over to the right of JoAnn's Fudge and then up on the second level. He'd gotten a fantastic rental deal from the owner, another freighter, who'd purchased a little house in the woods for him and his growing family. "Maybe we'll have to do the same one day," Jeremy had said recently to Cindy, who'd had to turn away to avoid showing her tears. Sometimes, grown-up stuff felt like too much to bear.

But this was real life. It was really happening.

She was in love.

As Tara and Tracey ambled into Jeremy's little apartment, Cindy grabbed her old-fashioned Canon camera and took candid photographs of them. Tara groaned, "This early in the morning? Can't you wait for me to look less like a zombie?"

"I told you. A real artist captures the in-between moments." Cindy laughed at herself, tossing her head back. "Not that I'm a real artist."

"It's not a hobby, either," Tracey affirmed, pouring herself a cup of coffee without asking. "You're good. Mom thinks you should have an exhibition. Something that captures island life."

"Island life. What does that even mean? This is normal life. Nothing special about it," Cindy countered.

Tara rolled her eyes toward Tracey. "She has no idea how the rest of the world operates."

"She's so privileged. Listen to her. She's in love with the handsome, Jeremy. She's a talented photographer. And on top of it, she's an islander without plans to even return to the mainland any time soon," Tracey teased.

"With a best friend who brings mimosas," Tara continued, drawing a bottle of champagne and a carton of orange juice from her JanSport backpack.

"You're kidding!" Cindy hugged her best friend as Tracey grabbed glasses from the cabinet, eyeing the dishwasher stains and scrubbing them clean.

Cindy had biscuits baking. The warm, buttery scent roared from the oven as she removed the baking sheet. Tracey stirred up overly alcoholic mimosas, saying they needed them to "guard against the cold."

"One shot is equal to one layer of clothing," Tara agreed in a mocking, scientific voice. "Everyone knows that."

As Tracey and Tara drank mimosas joyously, Cindy only pretended to. Luckily, her best friend and sister were soon already too tipsy to notice.

After a warm breakfast of egg sandwiches (using the biscuits as slices of bread), bacon, and potatoes, Cindy, Tara, and Tracey bundled up and headed out into the fresh chill of the mid-morning. Already, the Mackinac Winter Festival was mostly set up, with little stalls selling hot cider, hot cocoa, hot cider with rum, and hot mulled wine. Other vendors sold hot pretzels, corn dogs, chili, stews, and little fish sandwiches with homemade bread. Naturally, the fudge shops were already open— a Mackinac specialty, as they wanted to draw in tipsy revelers to buy their sugary treats.

As they walked through town, Cindy snapped several photographs of the islanders and tourists, capturing the spirit of the winter wonderland. Tara and Tracey gabbed with excitement, frequently joining in conversations with other islanders and vendors.

"Jeremy's racing today, isn't he?" a pretzel vendor asked Cindy.

"That's right."

"He's a master on the water. I can't imagine he won't be a master on ice, too."

Cindy laughed as a razor-sharp ray of sunshine flashed across her face. She lifted her eyes to find that the normal blanket of thick winter clouds rushed away to reveal a gorgeous blue sky.

"It's a beautiful day," another vendor reported.

The finish line for the Ice Bridge to Mackinac Island Race was located near the island's port. As the Ice Bridge wasn't for the faint of heart, it wasn't so much of a "race" as a "community get-together," with no real prize for first place and no real shame for last. Some riders were reportedly taking bikes across the ice as well, a feat Cindy deemed "silly" as it meant you were out in the whipping winds that much longer.

Cindy, Tara, and Tracey gathered out on the ferry docks to watch the first of the "racers" come in— snowmobiles, motorcycles, and bicycles, some of whom had probably begun their trek much earlier in the morning. The rest of the island gathered at the edge of the Michigan waters, waving flags and howling with excitement as they approached. A marching band, which stood at the bottom of Fort Mackinac, played classics badly, as their lips and fingers were frigid from the cold.

But that was the thing, wasn't it? The cold. *Was it really that cold?* Cindy watched as Tara removed her scarf and Tracey tore her hat from her head. Children removed their coats and flung themselves around in play, sweat billowing on their necks. There was a strangeness to this winter morning, a reminder that they had no real control over the wintery conditions. Yes, the meteorologist had said they'd remain below freezing that week. But what did a meteorologist really know about the future? Nobody could predict it.

A cyclist who came in about twenty-five minutes later was the first to indicate something was wrong.

"Ice cracking!" he yelled out as he jumped off his bike, allowing it to fall behind him. He pointed out across the menacing ice, where Christmas trees were lined up to mark the way. "Inside the Bridge. The ice is cracking!"

Cindy had a sinking feeling in the pit of her belly. Slowly, Tracy and Tara both grabbed her hands and held onto them, first gently and then harder. A hush came over the crowd as one of the race managers rushed up to the cyclist to ask him more questions, none of which Cindy could hear.

More racers came from the bridge, most looking shell-shocked. Their wives or girlfriends wrapped the men up with big blankets and led them off to their homes, past the vendors and past the celebration. There was a feeling of foreboding, a sense that whatever they'd set out to do that morning had a very different outcome than they'd planned. The band skittered away; music was unwanted and already forgotten.

There came the spitting sound of a helicopter up above, headed for the center of the Ice Bridge. More and more racers whipped over the racing line, none of whom were Jeremy. *And why not Jeremy?* He was one of the most confident riders Cindy knew. He'd whipped her around the island more times than she could count. He'd even driven her across the Ice Bridge two winters ago as she'd screeched with a mix of fear and joy.

"Let's wrap it up, folks!" One of the race organizers beckoned for everyone to step away from the docks and head back toward downtown.

It took a while to corral the islanders and tourists back toward the kiosks. When they returned, the islanders purchased hot wine, grateful for something to do with their hands. When they were finally forced away, Cindy walked with her shoulders hunched forward, her hands across her stomach.

"Cindy?" Another race organizer called for her, leafing her out of the rushing crowd. His eyes were tinged red with panic. "Cindy, would you mind coming over here for a second?"

Cindy dragged both Tara and Tracey along with her, latching her fingers around theirs. If they had let her go, Cindy would have collapsed across the cobblestones of the old-world island street. She would have fallen into the muck of the melting snow.

Already, within the hollowness of the race organizer's eyes, she knew the truth.

Jeremy wasn't coming home.

Chapter Two

One Year Later

The muffin top that crested over Cindy's jeans made every shirt in her closet drab-looking at best and all-out sloppy at worst. Standing in only a pair of jeans and a lace bra, she squeezed the thick fat and jiggled it, frowning in the wall-length mirror in her childhood bedroom. She was used to liking who she saw in that mirror— a teenage girl in tank tops, short skirts, and little flowery dresses. That girl didn't live there anymore.

"What did I tell you about that voice in your head?" Tara spoke from Cindy's bed, where she sat cross-legged in front of a big bowl of lightly salted popcorn, watching Cindy change outfits.

Cindy groaned and turned around, yanking her jeans higher on her hips. Her eyes scanned from Tara's beautiful face down to the little carrier on the floor next to the nightstand, where her five-month-old baby, Michael, slept peacefully, his little eyes darting around behind his eyelids. He was such a dreamer.

"I'm just not sure this is a good idea," Cindy breathed, dropping to her knees in front of Michael's carrier to adjust the blanket over his legs. He kicked gently but remained fast asleep.

"Why? Give me one good reason you shouldn't put yourself out there," Tara demanded.

Cindy roared. "Are you kidding me? I have about fifty good reasons."

Tara slipped toward the edge of her bed and dangled her feet over it. With a tender stroke of her hand, she drew a dirty blonde curl over Cindy's ear, just like Jeremy had done.

"You've been through hell and back, Cindy Swartz. Nobody deserved what happened to you. The love of your life left you and your baby behind. I'm not one of those people who says everything happens for a reason. I think it's up to us as humans to carry the weight of what has happened and find some way, somehow, to live with it. That said, I do think it's up for us to live as well as we can with the rest of the time we have left."

Cindy's throat tightened with sorrow. She leaned her head against Tara's palm and studied the beautiful porcelain skin of her darling son, who'd been born seven months after his daddy's death. The pregnancy had been her and Jeremy's little secret. And now, here he was: Michael Miller, a beautiful creature who was forced to live without the love his father had for him.

"I know you, Cindy. You won't be happy in this house on Pontiac Trail Head forever," Tara whispered. "Why not give this guy a shot?"

"What do we know about him?" Cindy murmured, sniffing slightly before bringing more force to her voice.

"He's a doctor of some kind," Tara reminded her. "Dermatologist, maybe? The kind of man who can give you and Michael a beautiful life."

Cindy bristled at the indication that Jeremy, with his freight liner salary, couldn't have. Tara quickly sensed this and corrected herself.

"That isn't to say Jeremy couldn't have built that with you, as well."

"It's okay. I understand what you mean. It's naive not to think that money isn't a part of the equation, especially if I want to get out from under my father's thumb," Cindy whispered. "And he's not an islander. Maybe that's for the best. No memories between us."

"Exactly. It's like you can start fresh."

Right before Cindy stepped out to meet the dermatologist, baby Michael began to wail in his carrier. Tara dropped down, cooing as she brought him into her arms. Cindy stood with her arms lifted, ready to care for her son. But Tara shooed her toward the door.

"I've got him, Cin."

"It's okay. If he's finicky today, I should just cancel."

"Cindy, go!" Tara looked formidable, all cheekbones and harsh eyes.

Cindy squeezed her son's foot gently, whispering, "I'll be home soon." She then made her way into the hallway and walked down the circular staircase, grateful that her sister, brother, mother, and father were tucked away in other rooms in the house on the hill. She didn't want to explain herself; she didn't want to say goodbye.

Fred Clemmens waited for Cindy at the table in the back corner of The Pink Pony. Two pints of beer sat sweating in front of him as he scanned the single television that hung over the bar. A basketball game played Michigan State versus Michigan, and he clutched the end of the table nervously as though he had a real idea of who he wanted to win.

From the doorway, Cindy analyzed him— this man she'd been set up with through friends of her father. *There's a new man on the island. A little older than your daughter, maybe. Looking for new friends if you know what I mean.*

It was a rare thing for people to just move to Mackinac Island without family or friends there. *Did it mean he was some kind of sociopath? Or did he just like the nature there— the majestic forests, white sandy beaches, and frothing waters off Lake Michigan and Lake Huron?*

At first glance, with his polo shirt and his khaki pants, Fred seemed like a sailor type. Guaranteed his occupation allowed him to purchase a sailboat for the upcoming spring and summer season. *Would Cindy be out on his boat? Would he eventually teach Michael the ropes?*

"Honey, are you going to sit down? Or what?" Marcy, the bartender in her late twenties or so, stepped out from behind the bar and gave Cindy a genuine, if confused, smile.

This caught Fred's attention. Cindy's cheeks burned red when he spotted her, giving her a once and then a twice-over. *Did he notice the muffin top beneath her sleek black dress? What about the extra layer of chub on her cheeks, which she hadn't managed fully to lose since Michael's birth?*

"Hi." Cindy's voice wavered as she greeted him.

Marcy spun back and nodded toward Fred as he stood. "Oh. You've already got a place. Did you decide on any snacks, Fred?"

Fred shook his head, his eyes still toward Cindy. "We're good for now, Marcy."

The air shimmered with intensity between them. Cindy stepped toward the corner table on wobbly legs, already imagining how she'd describe the scene to Tracey and Tara later. *"I've been at that bar about a thousand times, but this time, I felt like a stranger."*

But what was this intensity, exactly? It wasn't that the

conversation was particularly riveting, and it wasn't that Cindy wanted to throw herself into Fred's arms and kiss him with reckless abandon (like she'd done with Jeremy back in their teenage years).

Perhaps the intensity existed purely in the trauma of forcing herself back "out there"; perhaps it was because she was engaging with a human who wasn't her infant son, her best friend, or her sister. Or perhaps it was because once Cindy sat down at that table at the Pink Pony, she had a sense that her life was about to change for good.

"Thank you for already ordering me a beer," Cindy told him, although she normally preferred wine.

"I like to take care of things," Fred told her. "It's just one of my talents."

His voice was heavy with arrogance; his eyes danced with the light of the candle between them. After an abrupt pause, he smacked his palms together joyously at something that had happened on the television screen.

"That's right! Get 'em, boys!"

Cindy followed his gaze to the television to see that U of M was ahead of Michigan State. She shivered, remembering the big and ultra-cozy sweatshirt she'd always worn of Jeremy's. It had been Michigan State athletic wear, the team opposing Fred's.

"You're a U of M fan?" Cindy asked, taking a long sip of the light beer.

"That's right," Fred replied, his eyes still on the TV. "I went to undergrad and medical school there, which is a pretty rare accomplishment. Most people aren't good enough to stay at their undergrad for medical school, especially a place as prestigious as U of M. But you know, that means that I've spent the better part of my years hunkered down in a library in Ann Arbor."

"I'm sure there are worse places to be," Cindy suggested.

"Sure, but the minute I figured out I could open my practice on Mackinac..." Fred puffed out his cheeks dramatically. "I jumped at the chance."

Here, he pounded the table, his eyes on the basketball team. Cindy trained her eyes on the beer, thinking back to little Michael at home with Tara. *How old was Fred? Around thirty? A little older?* He gave off a similar air to her father, this know-how about the world. Cindy had never understood the world or its chaos. Jeremy, too, had admitted to being just about as lost as she was. "The freight line is simple. It's clean work. I know I'm needed there. Other careers? Selling things people don't need or going to school for a thousand years just to tell people what to do? I don't know if I could manage it," he'd told her. "It seems too fake to me."

The game ended about seven minutes later with a U of M win. Fred guzzled back his first beer and ordered them two more, even though Cindy was only halfway done with hers.

"Drink up. We're celebrating," he told her.

Cindy, who was normally in control of her life and her baby's life, alone in the world, did as she was told. It was nice for someone to take the reins for a change.

With a commercial break on television between basketball games, Fred turned his attention to Cindy. "You know, you're more beautiful than they said you were."

Cindy grimaced. "I have no idea who you mean by 'they.' And I have no idea if that's a compliment or not."

"It's a compliment," Fred told her. "How old are you? Twenty-one?"

"Twenty-three."

Cindy should have told him how rude it was to ask that kind of question. But with one beer down and very little food in her system, she couldn't rely on herself for a clever remark. She sipped her second beer and then forced herself to ask him simple questions to try to get to know him better.

"Where are you living?"

"I'm living above my dermatology practice until I figure out where I want to be long-term," Fred told her. "I have a life plan set out for myself. Goals I need to achieve before the age of thirty-three. A house. A wife... children."

Cindy's throat tightened. *Had the people who'd set them up mentioned her baby situation? How did Michael fit into this guy's strategic life plan?*

"Why thirty-three?" Cindy asked timidly.

Fred's grin was crooked and attractive, as though he'd stepped directly from the pages of a JCPenney catalog. Cindy's heart beat a little bit faster.

"I don't want to be an old dad," he told her. "My father was a lot older than me. He couldn't play catch with me in the backyard. Couldn't swim with me in Lake Erie. Didn't make it to my college graduation because he'd just had heart surgery."

"I'm sorry." Cindy furrowed her brows as she learned about his sorrows. Everyone had them. Even University of Michigan dermatology school graduates, apparently. Even men who seemed like they had the ability to make more money than God.

Midway through her second beer, Fred managed to take full control of the conversation, telling her nearly everything: about his five-year relationship in Ann Arbor that didn't work out, about his teenage belief that he could be a rock star, and about his love (of course) of sailing. Cindy was grateful to swim in his words and stories, nodding along and almost managing to forget her own sorrows.

After three beers, Fred announced that he planned to take her home but that he wanted to take her out for dinner in two nights. Cindy felt incredulous. *What had she brought to the conversation that he'd latched onto? What made him want to see her again?* It certainly wasn't the shadow of a muffin top beneath her black dress.

When Fred dropped her off at Pontiac Trail Head later that evening, he stood for a long moment in the frigid darkness, gazing out across the gorgeous Victorian homes. "This is where I want to raise my children," he announced. "It's the perfect place. Your father chose well."

Cindy's throat tightened at the mention of her father. *But then again, did she really want to raise Michael in some teensy, closet-sized apartment in downtown Mackinac? Didn't she want to have more children and watch them romp wildly in the backyard beneath the beautiful island sun?*

And what's more: didn't she want her children to have a good relationship with their grandparents, who would be just down the road?

"Looking forward to seeing you, Cindy," Fred told her, bowing his head. "I have had a pleasurable evening. One of the best in a long time."

It was difficult for Cindy to understand exactly why Fred Clemmens liked her at all. Tara insisted this was all due to Cindy's awful opinion of herself, which had taken a dramatic hit after Jeremy's death. "You never thought you were good enough for anyone. Jeremy just never listened to you. Maybe this guy won't, either," Tara pointed out.

After a second date and then a third with a fourth on the way, Cindy allowed herself to do something she hadn't been able to do in quite some time.

She allowed herself to hope.

With Tracey and Tara, she spoke specifically about this "hope" without mentioning anything concrete about the dates themselves. When asked more about Fred, she told the details: that he had a medical degree from the University of Michigan, that he wanted children, that he loved to sail, and that he'd had some longer-term failed relationships, kinds that had broken his heart.

"He sounds like a very real person," Tara said thoughtfully. "Like you've both come out of these separate stories to join forces."

"Yeah!" Cindy heard herself say, unsure if she fully believed it. "I'm going to tell him about Michael during the next date. It's time."

The following evening, Cindy and Fred met at a little pizza restaurant down the street from his dermatology office. There, Fred decided on a pepperoni pizza with onions and peppers. He then passed the menus back to the server without asking Cindy her opinion on the meal. Cindy's hands formed fists, but she kept them beneath the table, reminding herself that this was her chance to give Michael a great life. Plus, she liked pepperoni with onions and peppers. *Who didn't?*

Fred sipped his beer and eyed her lovingly. Cindy wanted to protest that he didn't even know her.

"Fred, I have to tell you something." It was only about thirty seconds after Fred had placed the order. *Was it too soon? When was the correct time to tell your new beau that you had a child with the love of your life who was now deceased?*

Fred froze, save for a little patch on his cheek that twitched.

"The thing is..." Cindy began. "I already um. I have a..."

"Is this about your son?" Fred asked.

It was Cindy's turn to freeze. She blinked, her eyes widening as Fred gave her a strained smile.

"You must know what a tiny place Mackinac is," Fred told her. "I've known about your little bundle of joy since before I met you."

"But you still agreed to meet me?" Cindy asked, her voice wavering slightly.

Fred shrugged. "You're probably more ready to have a family than most."

Ah. Was Fred's growing love for her purely based on logistics?

"Plus, you're still one of the most beautiful and... kind women on Mackinac..."

The stuttered pauses between his words gave Cindy pause. She sipped her beer and shoved away a strange instinct to get the hell out of there as fast as she could.

"I'd like you to meet him," she said finally.

"How old?"

"Almost six months."

Fred's dark hair had been styled back with gel. It looked as though he'd specifically taken each strand, one at a time, and layered it across his skull. It was a level of vanity Cindy could hardly understand.

"And his name?"

"Michael. Michael Miller," Cindy responded.

"His father's last name."

"That's right." Cindy took a massive gulp of beer to ease her nerves.

The pizza arrived, shining with grease. The pepperoni slabs were heavy with it, curving down to create little pools. Fred grabbed a napkin and began to sop up the grease, saying that he'd seen the damage oil like that did to the skin.

"If you marry a dermatologist," he explained with a laugh, "You'll have some of the best skin on this island. I can guarantee that. I'll keep you looking brand new."

People got involved with people for all sorts of reasons. Cindy's high school friend Monica had married her husband just because he'd inherited a mini fortune from his grandfather. A celebrity Cindy had read about in a tabloid magazine had married his wife because she'd beaten him at poker.

Was it so bad to marry someone who promised to care for

you and your son, to buy a house a few down from your parents, and to care for you (and your skin) all the days of your life?

His arrogance was like a heavy blanket of clouds, blocking out the light of everything else.

But it's not like Cindy remembered what light felt like, anyway. Not since Jeremy's death.

Later that night, Cindy placed Michael gently into Fred's arms as he sat perched at the edge of her childhood bed. Michael kicked his little feet out, squirming so much that Fred said, "Maybe he's a little athlete."

There was a sterile quality to the way Fred held Michael that evening. But Cindy told herself that the sterility came purely from Fred's lack of experience with children. He'd repeatedly said that he wanted children. He wanted to do it with her, Michael included.

"This is the path forward," Cindy told Tara over the phone after Fred left. "I can feel it."

Still, she never translated her doubts about Fred.

When Tara met Fred for the first time, she verbalized her real opinions, the arrogance and darkness she felt behind his eyes. To this, Cindy simply said, "I'm happy. And as my best friend, it's up to you to be happy for me." They were words she'd rehearsed to herself in the mirror, words she carried with her like a beacon until she walked down the aisle. "I'm happy," she whispered to herself. "I'm just so happy, and I never imagined I could be this happy again."

She prayed that one day soon, she'd fully believe herself.

Chapter Three

Present-Day

For many years after Jeremy Miller's accident at the Ice Bridge Race, Mackinac Island officials canceled the race and declared riding across the Ice Bridge "illegal" when temperatures went above a certain level. Just because the race was no more, however, didn't mean that the Ice Bridge didn't take its fair share of tourists, many of whom lost their way at night and rode their snowmobiles directly into the icy darkness of Lake Michigan.

But tragedy was easily forgotten.

By the time Michael was fifteen years old, the Ice Bridge Race was reinstated, drawing tourists and locals alike to the St. Ignace to Mackinac Ice Bridge Race, which culminated in a glorious Winter Festival. Lucky for Cindy, Michael had never been particularly drawn to winter sports and spent most of the hours of the Ice Bridge Race at home with his high school friends, playing cards or video games and stealing what they could of Fred's beer. "I like water sports," Michael explained once within earshot of Cindy. "But out there on the ice? Tempting fate? No thanks."

Cindy had made it her mission since the accident twenty-five years ago to get as far away from the Winter Festival and Ice Bridge Race as she could. Even the smell of the mulled wine and the sound of the marching band, all lined up on the hill below the Fort, dragged her back into her previous terrors. Memory was a strange and volatile thing. She'd made it her life's mission to fight it.

On the morning of this February's Ice Bridge Race, Cindy stood in a terrycloth robe and, a pair of slippers and watched the drip-drip of the coffee as it fell into the pot. Down the hall, behind a closed door, Fred sat in front of the television, catching up on the weeks' sporting events. He'd just sent her a text demanding a cup of coffee.

Cindy spread her hands out on the cool marble of the kitchen counter. As the coffee dribbled, she closed her eyes and tried, for the first time in a long, long time, to picture what it had been like to stand in Jeremy's kitchen in downtown Mackinac. That last morning at his apartment, when he'd already run off to start the Ice Bridge race. *What had it smelled like? What had the tiles felt like beneath her feet? Where had he kept the mugs, the bowls, or the single wine glass? And what had they played on that little radio?*

God, it had been so long since she'd even been able to picture Jeremy's face. *What might he have looked like twenty-five years later?* He was frozen in youth, his muscles constantly round, hearty, and his smile generous and easy.

What was she doing, drudging back these old memories? She snapped her eyes open, poured Fred a mug of coffee, then walked down the hallway, just as Fred howled expletives at the television. When she opened the door to place the mug of coffee on the little table alongside the couch, Fred didn't twitch his head even an inch to say hello.

"Idiots don't know what hit 'em," he said of the opposite team.

"Aren't these just the highlights from last night?" Cindy countered.

Fred ignored her, just as he often did on Saturday mornings. He'd once told her Saturday mornings were "alone time" for him, essential after his long week of work.

No wonder Michael never comes around anymore.

The thought smacked the back of Cindy's mind like a rogue tennis ball. She closed the door to Fred's TV room and returned to the kitchen to grab herself a mug of coffee, into which she poured the slightest bit of Bailey's. As she sipped, she tried to think of the last time Fred had looked at her, really looked at her.

A knock at the front door forced Cindy out of her reverie. When she opened it, she discovered Tracey and Elise carrying a large box of donuts from the local donut shop in downtown Mackinac, plus a paper bag of what Tracey called "necessary supplies to get through this crazy day."

Tracey swallowed Cindy up in a hug as Elise hovered beside them, holding both the bag of alcohol and the box of donuts. For a moment, Cindy felt a strange swell of rage at Elise being there at all. Elise— and not Tara, Cindy's best friend.

Time had really had its way with all of them, hadn't it?

But it wasn't Elise's fault.

Not Elise's fault that her mother had had an affair with Dean Swartz all those years ago.

Not Elise's fault that Tara had died in that terrible car accident off the island.

Not Elise's fault that she'd fallen in love with Tara's widower, Wayne.

Not Elise's fault, either, that she and Wayne had become

very close with Michael since Michael's return to the island after three years away.

Not Elise's fault at all.

"I guess you've heard about this very particular time for me..." Cindy breathed as she stepped back from Tracey's hug and addressed Elise.

"Don't worry. I told her it's not something we talk about in mixed company," Tracey said. "Although I still think..."

"I still don't see any reason why we should drag Michael through the mess of all that," Cindy stated. She then snapped her eyes back to Elise and muttered, "Fred and I just thought it was easier never to tell him when he was younger."

"And now, he's twenty-four years old and still doesn't know his father's identity?" Elise murmured, her eyes widening with surprise.

"He left when he was twenty-one. We had no idea he planned to come back," Cindy offered pointedly, as though that was any kind of answer.

Cindy stepped around Elise, sensing that this story punched a very familiar bruise within Elise. Elise had only just come to Mackinac the previous autumn on a hunch that her mother had met her father and conceived Elise there. But there was a difference between Elise's and Michael's stories. Unlike Elise, Michael had had a father since he was a baby. That father was Fred Clemmens.

Fred had even adopted him right out of the gate, insisting that they were a complete family.

The fact that they hadn't been able to have any other children after Megan, their daughter, hadn't exactly thrilled him, though. Although he'd never said it out loud, Fred had always wanted a son all his own. Michael, another man's son, just didn't cut it.

And the two had never really gotten along since.

Tracey grabbed a bottle of champagne from the bottom of

the brown paper bag and stirred up mimosas for the three of them. Elise cupped her elbows nervously, her eyebrows slightly furrowed. Cindy could tell that Elise was heavy with questions about why Cindy had never told her son the truth. *But how could Cindy explain the complexities of that long-ago time? How could she explain the nuances of her marriage to Fred?*

"Shall we toast?" Tracey asked, lifting her sparkling mimosa toward the other two.

Cindy and Elise grabbed the stems of their drinks and lifted them, both watching Tracey.

"I never know what to say on this day every year," Tracey began. "How best can we honor that beautiful, kind, and generous man, Jeremy Miller?"

Cindy's eyes filled with tears. She blinked them back quickly as down the hall, Fred hollered something at the television. Tracey and Elise exchanged glances as Elise whispered, "Is Fred here?"

"Yeah. But he never comes out of that room," Cindy explained.

"It's still bad vibes," Tracey returned, scrunching her nose.

Again, Fred roared down the hallway. Cindy sipped her mimosa, ending Tracey's speech before it even got a proper start. Elise stared at the counter.

"Remember that morning? When I made those other, much stronger mimosas? And you just pretended to drink them?" Tracey tried.

"Oh gosh. Pregnancy?" Elise tried to smile.

"Just my little secret," Cindy whispered. "The doctor said it was a miracle I didn't miscarry from all the stress."

"Michael is a miracle baby," Tracey affirmed, trying to brighten the mood.

"Just a great guy," Elise said. "Wayne loves splitting all the work with him at the coffee shop. He says he sees him as a younger brother. We had him over for dinner the other night."

Tracey's eyes found Elise's again; they urged her to quit. Elise snapped her lips closed again, then sipped her mimosa.

Cindy's heart felt bruised. "It's okay, Elise. You can talk about him."

Elise pressed the tips of her fingers against her lips. After a long pause, she whispered, "I'm sorry. I feel like I just keep saying the wrong thing."

"It's not your fault that my son won't talk to me," Cindy reminded both Elise and herself.

Elise shrugged her right shoulder timidly. "I think just, you know. After that last fight with Fred he had, and after Margot left him..."

"Margot left him?" Cindy gasped.

Margot had appeared on Mackinac Island the previous autumn with a Texas twang and a sincere love for Michael Clemmens, whom she'd met at a coffee shop in Texas on Michael's mad three-year journey across the continent. During those initial months after Michael's return, the family had fallen into an easy rhythm, with Michael and Margot frequently stopping in for birthday dinners and other family get-togethers. That hadn't lasted.

"I didn't know you didn't know," Elise murmured, recognizing that she'd screwed up again.

"Why don't we go outside for a walk?" Tracey waved a hand toward the window, where snow sloped dramatically from one end of the backyard to the other, glittering in the bright February light. The thermometer that hung on the window said the temperature was eleven degrees Fahrenheit—cold enough, certainly. The ice would hold.

A little while later, Elise, Tracey, and Cindy walked their bundled-up forms along the trails behind the Pontiac Trail Head. They were quiet, listening to the twittering of the birds and the crunch of their feet on the first layer of snow. It had been a particularly wet winter, layering them with many feet of snow. On the island, it wasn't like anyone needed to get anywhere fast; snow wasn't a detriment, as it was anywhere else. It just added a little flavoring.

"Did you ever talk about Jeremy to anyone?" Elise asked timidly. "Like a therapist?"

Cindy dug her hands deeper into her pockets. Above them, a cardinal landed on a branch, making it tilt to-and-fro.

"No," Cindy finally answered. "I never really saw a reason to."

Elise and Tracey exchanged glances again. Cindy almost called them out on it. It was like they'd had some conversation about this prior to meeting her. *We have to convince Cindy to make herself mentally healthier.*

"Fred offered me a way out," Cindy continued after a dramatic pause.

"Just because you and Fred created a life together doesn't mean that what happened to you doesn't have any effect," Tracey began.

Cindy wanted to howl, *you think I don't know that?* But she kept her lips closed tight. She was Midwestern, after all.

"When I stared the truth of my life in the face last autumn, I was finally able to make sense of so much," Elise confessed tentatively. "I was finally able to put the puzzle pieces together."

"And you've watched the way Dad's opened up," Tracey pointed out. "Now that Elise is here and he's able to talk about himself and his life with more honesty, he's become happier. Lighter even."

Cindy flared her nostrils. "I didn't expect an ambush today, girls."

There was another pause.

Tracey sighed, dropping her shoulders forward as she muttered, "I just don't want this sorrow to keep growing like cancer. I hate that Fred has basically allowed you to delete Jeremy from your heart and your mind."

"I obviously still think about him!" Cindy cried. Tears threatened to fall from the corners of her eyes.

"Of course, you do," Tracey muttered. "He was the love of your life."

"Actually, Fred is," Cindy pointed out firmly. "He raised Michael and Megan with me. He stayed by me in sickness and in health. He paid the mortgage; he paid for vacations; he put food to eat on the table. If that isn't the love of my life, then I don't know who is."

"Of course," Elise quickly agreed. "We didn't mean to be rude."

Cindy's phone buzzed through Cindy's pocket. She pulled it out to discover Fred's name across the front.

"Hi, honey. I'm out for a walk with the girls."

Fred sounded both disgruntled and distracted, as though she'd been the one to call him. The television continued to blare in the background. Cindy could practically still feel his eyes burned to the screen.

"I just checked the fridge. We're out of those wings."

Cindy closed her eyes as the colossal ache of this phone call hammered into her. Fred had great timing. "I can stop at the store to pick some up."

Again, Elise and Tracey looked as though they had a whole lot to say. Cindy turned away from them, burning with embarrassment. Her boots scuffed through the snow.

"I'll just head downtown then," Fred coughed into the phone.

Cindy's head donged like a bell. "What do you mean?"

"I mean, I'll head down to the festival to get some food and beer," Fred returned.

In all her years of marriage to Fred, Cindy had never known Fred to go out of his way to go down to the Ice Bridge

Race. He normally respected her wishes to avoid the festivities altogether.

Yet here he was, on his way out.

Like punishment for not having the wings in the fridge.

"Okay..." Cindy began, hardly able to hear herself. Her knees clacked together.

"Yep. No need to take care of anything around the house, Cindy. I can take care of myself."

With that, Fred hung up the phone.

When Cindy turned back to her sister and half-sister, she pressed her phone hard against her chest and swallowed several times to get the lump out of her throat. She'd never felt so foolish.

"We need more mimosas," she told them. "Maybe we can head to your place, Tracey? Such a cozy little place."

Elise and Tracey nodded, jumping forward to lace their arms through Cindy's and guide her back down the hill toward Tracey's little humble home, where she'd raised her daughter, Emma, without a single man in tow. Cindy respected her for that. She'd never been half as strong.

Chapter Four

It was mid-April, but so close to the Upper Peninsula of Michigan, it might as well have still been in the dark depths of February. This was the life of a Michigander. Sweating slightly in her four layers of clothing, Cindy held her umbrella strategically, trying to catch the balls of hail that slid sideways from the sky above. She was steps from her daughter Megan's apartment in downtown Mackinac, directly above the fudge shop where she worked. It was two apartments away from the one she'd shared with Jeremy Miller all those years ago. Megan had no clue.

Megan pulled the door open joyously as Cindy approached. She was the spitting image of Mandy, Cindy's mother who'd died nearly three years ago, with a smile that seemed to crack open instantaneously at the slightest hint of gladness. It was a wonder that Megan was Fred's "real" child. Emotionally, she didn't resemble him at all.

"Hi, honey." Cindy collapsed her umbrella and stepped inside as her daughter closed the door carefully.

"That hail came out of nowhere," Megan cried.

"It came out of the Michigan sky," Cindy joked. "You know that. You're a Michigan girl, through and through."

Megan was wearing a pair of baggy jeans, a black t-shirt, and a pair of fuzzy socks. On the table beside her second-hand couch sat several books, including one that was wide open to the page she'd been reading when Cindy had arrived. The lamp in the corner had belonged to her Grandma Mandy. It was the same lamp Mandy had read under for the better part of thirty-five years.

"I have some bad news," Megan announced, her voice in a sing-song tone.

"Uh oh."

Cindy followed her daughter into the little kitchen, where Megan had several pots mid-boil. She placed a wooden spoon in a big pot of goop and scraped the bottom to drag up a lot of black.

"I wanted to make curry," Megan said with a sigh, showing off the disgusting spoon. "But I got really invested in my book and lost track of time."

"Oh no!" Cindy laughed good-naturedly. "I've never made that before."

"I know. I wanted to impress you. Guess I failed." Megan turned the knobs to OFF on the stovetop, checked her phone, then said, "But the lunch specials at The Grind have been killer lately."

Cindy's stomach twisted itself into knots. She leaned against the kitchen wall, eyeing the calendar on the opposite wall, upon which Megan and her cousin, Emma, had listed out all the events of the upcoming weeks. DENTIST APPOINTMENT. PARTY AT RICK'S. TRAINING AT WORK. (FUDGE 4 LYFE.)

"I don't know, honey." Cindy sighed.

Megan dropped one of the gunk-filled pots into the sink and turned on the water to fill it to the brim. "You and Michael not talking affects more than just you and Michael, you know."

Cindy crossed her arms tighter over her chest so that she could feel her heart pounding through her forearms.

"You don't even have to say more than hi to each other," Megan continued. "I just think it's ridiculous that you can't just go to, like, the only good coffee shop in town, just because of some stupid family fight."

A few minutes later, Cindy found herself following her daughter down Main Street, headed for the coffee shop that Michael now operated with Wayne, his makeshift "adoptive brother." Wayne and Michael had always, always been close—even before Michael had headed out for his cross-country journey. Tara and Wayne had been Michael's makeshift parents, as though Michael had sensed in his bones that Fred didn't belong to him.

Tara had never given the news away. She'd taken it to her grave.

The Grind was busy as ever, proof that it really was the first stop for most islanders at lunchtime. Wayne and Michael flew around the back of the counter, heating up quiches, preparing cappuccinos, placing scones on china plates, and chatting with customers. Cindy hadn't seen Michael's face in a good three months, and the sight of it now was striking— a strong, handsome jawline, thick black hair, and eyes that reminded her terribly of Jeremy.

Michael was his ghost.

"Why don't you sit down, and I'll order for us?" Megan told her mother.

Cindy nodded, knowing this was the best way forward, even if it made her feel about ten inches tall. She headed for the corner of The Grind to an empty booth. Leftover mugs remained, which Wayne soon hustled over to collect. As he smeared a rag across the table, he greeted her warmly and said,

"I haven't seen you in The Grind in quite a while, Miss Cindy."

"Megan was bragging about your lunch specials."

"The quiche and soup combo today are killer," he told her. "Michael's been experimenting with recipes the past few months, ever since Margot..." He winced and glanced back toward Michael, who was in a vibrant conversation with his sister, Megan. "I don't know. You can't tell by looking at him, but he's really broken up about Margot leaving him. I never saw it coming."

"Twenty-somethings," Cindy said with a shrug. "I guess you can't expect that they'll stay together forever."

"I don't know. I met Tara in my twenties," Wayne pointed out. "And you met Fred."

"True." Cindy dropped her gaze to the table, praying that Megan would join her shortly. Every second was a reminder that Cindy hardly knew her son at all. Megan's laughter rollicked across the already-noisy coffee shop. Michael could be hilarious; Cindy knew it well. He'd gotten it from Jeremy.

Megan appeared at the back booth a few minutes later with two cappuccinos, two glasses of water, and a receipt that read: **2 X QUICHE SOUP SPECIALS**. She beamed with joy after her conversation with her brother.

"Michael looks good," Cindy commented, dropping her lips over the edge of the coffee mug so that milky foam came over her tongue.

"He said the same thing about you."

Cindy countered. "Yeah, right."

"You have to stop thinking of yourself like that," Megan shot back.

Cindy was reminded of what Tara used to say: that Cindy had to be conscious of the negative voice in the back of her head, telling her she wasn't enough.

"It's nice to watch you and your brother laugh like that,"

Cindy expressed after a few moments. "Feels like I haven't laughed like that in a long time."

Megan couldn't lift her eyes to meet Cindy's. "I hate to hear you say that."

Cindy shrugged. "I don't know. Maybe when you're forty-seven years old, the way I am, the time for laughs is over."

"I hope not." Megan's words were terribly quiet, as though she spoke at a funeral.

Cindy cursed herself for being in such a dark mood. Her daughter had wanted to have an upbeat lunch with her to catch up after not seeing one another for a week. Although she lived just downtown, Megan's schedule had been work-heavy as of late, with her taking over operations for training the newest fudge sellers at the downstairs fudge shop.

"Tell me about the training sessions," Cindy finally heard herself say.

At this, Megan rolled her eyes the slightest bit, as though this was the most ridiculous thing she'd ever been asked to do. After another pregnant pause, she began to describe what she had to do as a trainer at the fudge shop. Not a single of her descriptions sounded passionate. It was like she'd turned into a zombie.

After lunch, Megan planned to meet up with her cousin Emma at a friend's place up the hill. This left Cindy with an entire afternoon at her disposal. As she stepped out toward the front door, she eyed the front counter of The Grind, hunting for Michael. He was in back somewhere, tending to the scones or counting the money or performing some other managerial duty. Her heart swelled to know that she still wouldn't talk to him that day. Perhaps they never would again.

With Megan off to the races of her life, Cindy wandered

through downtown in a daydream state. She eyed the top window of the apartment where she and Jeremy had once lived, trying yet again to visualize who they'd been all those years ago. Michael had been conceived there.

As she continued to walk westward, back toward Pontiac Trail Head, she nearly ran headlong into a man she almost recognized. Cindy jumped off to the left, surprised at herself for not paying attention and splaying her hand across her chest with a dramatic, "Oh my! Pardon me."

The man was, in a word, handsome, even in his fifty-some years. He stood in a pair of khakis and a button-down shirt with his hands clasped behind his back as he analyzed the massive still-dead bush that hung over the fence near downtown.

After a moment, Cindy realized who this man was.

"Oh! You're Ron. Ron Waters," Cindy said excitedly. "We've never met personally, but gosh, I have to tell you that I really admire your work."

Ron's eyes shimmered with happiness at the compliment. He bowed his head, showing a bright bald spot in the center, and said, "And you're Cindy Clemmons."

Cindy laughed. "The island is small, even for you who only live here part-time."

"Actually, I spent some of the winter here," Ron told her. "I wanted to see what it felt like to see the seasons change."

"And what did you think?"

"It was..." He considered this, a smile playing out across his lips. "Cold. In a word, cold. But other than that, I really appreciated it. Beautiful, as ever. And I think I'll appreciate spring that much more because of it."

Cindy beamed up at him, all six-foot-three of him. She had the strangest sensation that she flirted with him, that she was a teenager on the verge of asking a boy to go out. How stupid. She was forty-seven and married.

"I guess you're doing the Lilac Festival again this year?" Cindy asked him.

"That's why I'm in front of this bush." Ron gestured toward the still-dead plants. "I want to make sure all our most vibrant bushes are ready to come back this spring. It's essential to the nature of the festival. Otherwise, we have to get busy with planting."

"This one looks pretty good." Cindy stepped toward it, analyzing the little nubs on the still-black twigs. "It's one of the bigger ones at the festival, isn't it?"

"And therefore, very important," Ron affirmed.

Cindy's smile widened. "I give this one a ninety-five percent chance of coming back."

"And you're someone to be trusted with these things?"

"Well," Cindy began, "My garden is one of my bigger passions, I guess. As lame as that sounds."

Ron's eyes widened. "Not in the slightest bit lame. There's a real beauty to building and growing a garden. It's like your own personal universe. I began to think of the Lilac Festival that way. All these little unique bushes." He shook his head. "But it's so much pressure, with so many thousands of people coming to the island to see them. The tourism industry rests on my shoulders right now. And in the midst of this terrible April weather, I feel a whole lot of worry."

"I don't think you should," Cindy told him. "It's just because you spent winter here. It's still in your bones. Spring is spring, just as it always has been before. And your Lilac Festival will flourish."

"I hope you're right." Ron placed his tongue against the inside of his cheek so that it bulged out, making him look silly, almost like a very tall child. He then added, "You know, I'm looking for people to work the festival this year. People who have a unique love for gardening."

Cindy's heart skipped at least two beats.

"If you have the time, that is," Ron continued.

"I think I can make time," Cindy told him, despite knowing that her schedule was wide open, save for the breakfasts, lunches, and dinners she had to make for Fred. "I really welcome this idea, Ron. I think I need to watch the lilacs bloom this year, maybe even more than ever before."

Chapter Five

WAYNE: Hey Cindy! You're invited tonight to dinner at my place.

WAYNE: I hope you and Fred can make it.

It was a few days after the fateful lunch at The Grind. With her cell across her palm, Cindy stood on the treadmill in the downstairs "gym room," which she and Fred had set up about fifteen years ago to dedicate themselves to their health and their waistlines. (In truth, she was half-sure that Fred had wanted the treadmill to make sure Cindy stayed "trim" despite middle age, but Cindy didn't like to think about that. As a dermatologist with almost perfect skin and ever-perfect muscles, despite nearing sixty years old, Fred was allowed to be judgemental. Maybe.)

A dinner. At Wayne's place.

Why?

Cindy's thoughts chased themselves around as she ramped up the speed of the treadmill, running herself toward delirium. *Did he want to play "good cop" and try to get Cindy and Michael to make amends? Or did this have nothing at all to do with Michael?* She pressed the STOP button, which made the treadmill stall in a flash, and then called Tracey to confirm.

"Yep. I'm invited, too," Tracey told her. "And Emma."

"What do you think it's for?" Cindy asked. Sweat rolled down the back of her neck and pooled against her t-shirt.

"I don't know, Cindy. I guess Wayne likes us and is dating our half-sister or something..." Tracey said, her voice laced with sarcasm. "Is that not enough for you?"

"I'm just scared that Michael will be there," Cindy said, restarting the treadmill manically to a steady three miles an hour, a perfect walker's pace.

"He will be," Tracey replied, her words like a metaphorical shrug. "But isn't it time for you guys to just... get over it? I mean, come on. It's Michael, Cindy. You love Michael more than life itself."

"I know that," Cindy barked back. "But he doesn't. Plain and simple."

"You're both too proud," Tracey returned. "I don't know what to do with either of you. I'm bringing an extra bottle of wine to make it through the night."

When Cindy reported to Fred what their night's plan was, he wasn't entirely thrilled. She gently reminded him that, back in the old days, he and Wayne had gotten along pretty well. Fred snorted at this, saying that Wayne and Fred had never seen eye-to-eye. (This was totally false. In fact, Tara, Cindy, Wayne, and Fred had gotten on like gangbusters for years, back in the old days, drinking and laughing on the back porch of Fred and Cindy's house.)

"And Michael will be there," she added.

"What do I care about that?" Fred demanded.

"He's your son."

The shock of her words filtered out through the air. Fred

blinked at her through the haze of the TV room, then cackled gently.

"If you say so," he told her.

* * *

Cindy and Fred arrived at Wayne's place around seven that evening, thirty minutes before dinner was served. "Lasagna," Wayne explained, wrapping a hand around Elise's waist, and beaming down at her. "Elise has the best recipe, it turns out. I thought California girls only ate avocados and drank lemon water."

"You've got a lot to learn about California girls," Elise teased him. She splayed a handout as she asked the newly arrived guests, "Can I take your coats?"

Fred and Cindy, the boring and quiet married couple, gave over their coats, which Elise took to the back bedroom. It was eerie for Cindy to be there, in the beautiful little place where Wayne and Tara had lived their lives together. Could Wayne just transplant Elise into Tara's spot?

Oh, but wasn't that so cruel of Cindy to think? Elise was her half-sister, after all— a truly beautiful and kind human who'd gone through so many traumas of her own. She hadn't asked for any of this. And didn't Wayne and Elise both deserve to fall in love again?

Cindy had thought she'd deserved that all those years ago when she'd begun to date Fred after Jeremy's accident. It was selfish to think Wayne and Elise didn't deserve it, too.

Cindy sat nervously on Wayne's couch in front of the fireplace, rubbing the edges of her skirt distractedly. A photograph on the mantle illustrated a beautiful memory between Elise and Wayne in front of the Christmas tree, their arms wrapped around one another as Elise lifted her chin toward his for a Christmas kiss. Where had Wayne put all the photographs of

Tara? Cindy had one directly on her desk in the upstairs study, a photo of Tara and Cindy on the single trip they'd taken to Florida together. They'd been thirty years old, Cindy with two kids at home and Tara in the initial throes of learning she couldn't have kids. *"I've wanted to be a mother my entire life, Cindy. I don't know what to do with the hollowness in my heart."*

"Can I get you a drink, Cindy?" Elise hovered to the side of the couch with her hands clasped together.

"What? Oh. Um." Cindy strung her tongue along the backs of her teeth.

"I'm having white wine," Elise said. "If that sounds good?"

"Sure. Perfect."

"And Fred? A beer?"

Fred offered a grunt that meant "yes," then collapsed on the couch next to Cindy. He tossed a handful of mixed nuts between his teeth and crunched obstinately. As Elise poured Cindy a glass of wine, she and Wayne exchanged glances, probably thinking, *Lucky us. Cindy and Fred came first.*

"The place looks good, Wayne," Cindy tried. A proper Midwestern woman could compliment her way out of any awkward situation.

"Thanks!" Wayne's voice sounded forced. "Elise has helped with a lot of the decorating. When she took me out to LA to see her place, I knew I needed to get to work if I wanted to keep her here on the island."

"All that space," Elise said, shaking her head. "I never needed it. My ex-husband and I got caught up in the rat race of living in the big city. I can't tell you how many hours I spent vacuuming and mopping and dusting that big, stupid house. Turns out, I like the coziness of this place much better."

"Yes, but you nearly lost your mind at the paint color in the bathroom," Wayne teased her.

"You're right. There were essential changes to be made." Elise's smile was delicate, like an unfurling flower in spring.

"And I'm sure you have a whole list of other changes up your sleeves." Wayne selected two cashews and an almond from the bowl of mixed nuts on the side table. "If I know anything about you Swartz women, it's that you have an eye for details."

He eyed Cindy, trying to tease her. Cindy lifted the corners of her mouth to attempt a smile. Fred coughed, maybe choking on a nut. Just then, there was a knock on the door, and both Elise and Wayne hustled away, grateful to do anything else but make small talk with them.

"There he is!" Wayne hollered joyously as the next guest entered. There was the sound of Wayne smacking him on the back, then the response from none other than Cindy's first child, Michael.

"You make it sound like we didn't just spend all day together at the coffee shop."

"He's always so happy to see me," Wayne joked, stepping back to allow Michael to enter.

Cindy craned her head back to watch Michael step through the foyer, stalling slightly as his eyes locked with his mother's. "Hi, there."

"Hey." Cindy lifted herself from the couch to turn toward her son, who carried a bottle of fancy wine in the crook of his arm.

Fred hardly glanced back, maybe to try to avoid the simmering tension between Cindy and Michael. Elise bustled in after Michael and set to work, pouring Michael a glass of red wine.

"I just can't believe how busy it's been up at The Grind lately. I can hardly get a table up there these days. And it's not even summer yet!" Elise continued as she pressed the glass into Michael's hands.

"They just come for Michael's good looks," Wayne countered.

"Are you saying that they don't come for my stellar service?" Michael asked, flashing him a teasing grin.

"Come for the Michael, stay for the service." Wayne cackled at his own joke.

"The older ladies on the island don't come there for me," Michael teased.

"I keep telling you to go for Miss Josephine," Wayne said, referring to an elderly lady who'd been a forever islander. "She just lights up when you're around."

Michael's gaze quivered toward Cindy's. *Did Michael think that Cindy remained in the dark about his girlfriend leaving him on the island and heading back to Texas? Did he want her to be in the dark about it?* Cindy sucked down more of her wine as anxiety crashed through her.

The horror of being alone in a room with Michael, Elise, and Wayne soon dissipated as other guests arrived. First came Megan, who fell between her mother and father on the couch and spoke to them excitedly, passing them each little slivers of fudge. This brightened Fred's mood considerably. Shortly after, Tracey and Emma stepped through the door, as did Wayne's sister, Sarah, with her two teenage daughters, Libby and Ashley. Last came Alex and their father, Dean, along with his golden retriever, Diesel. Alex and Elise hugged somberly, still overcoming the tumultuous first few months of their relationship.

The living room became vibrant and chaotic, with no fewer than five stories being told at any given time. Cindy's ear struggled to catch any one story and instead jumped from Megan's to Emma's to Elise's. Dean sat at the head of the dining room table already, nursing a glass of wine and speaking in gritty yet amicable tones to Wayne. After the death of their mother, the widowers Wayne and Dean had fallen into a warm and nourishing friendship, leaning on one another through the dark eras of loneliness.

Cindy finished her first glass of wine a little too quickly. Unsure of what to do with her hands, she stood and refilled her glass, grateful that nobody seemed to notice. As she sipped, the oven timer beeped, drawing Wayne into the kitchen to remove the lasagna and announce it was nearly time to eat.

It was difficult to decide who sat where.

Fred, never one to be told what to do, sat at the head of the table across from Dean. Michael sat next to his grandfather, fluttering a napkin across his lap. A part of Cindy dared her to just go up to her son and sit next to him, ask him how he was. But another part told her that would be tremendously awkward for all involved. *And what if Michael just got up and moved chairs? Would she ever get over it?*

Fear dropped Cindy into the chair beside her husband. Megan sat across from her, sighing about how beautiful the food looked.

"I haven't eaten much more than fudge and salad all week long," she said with a laugh.

"We need to get better about cooking," Emma suggested.

"If you feel so passionate about it, I'll let you take over the meal planning," Megan shot back.

"Oh gosh. When you're twenty-one and twenty-two, I guess you can get by with Snickers for dinner." The last light of the day caught Elise's blonde curls as she tossed her head back joyously, laughing with Emma and Megan as though she'd always been a part of the family.

Suddenly, Wayne splayed a hand across his forehead and let out a low sigh. Everyone at the table turned toward him, conscious that the mood had shifted.

"I'm sorry," Wayne sighed. "You've all got food on your plates that you want to eat and wine in your glasses you want to drink. I told myself I would let the party go on a little while longer before..."

He trailed off. Tracey caught Cindy's gaze over the table, her eyes as big as eggs. The air filled yet again with tension.

Wayne shoved his chair back, dug into the pocket of his black jeans, and removed a little black velvet box. Wordless, Elise brought her hands to her cheeks as Wayne dropped to one knee, laughing a bit as he went.

"That is the sound of a very old man trying his hand at being in love again," Wayne said, his crooked smile stretching across his left cheek.

"You don't get to say you're old till you get to be my age," Dean countered.

Wayne laughed nervously, drawing his eyes toward Elise's. After a long and ponderous pause, he said, "Elise. For many years, I never thought I could make my way out of the darkness. Every day seemed like this heavy weight on my shoulders. I would ask myself, how can I possibly go on like this? Without hope? Without love? Without any plan? And then, one day at the ferry docks in Mackinaw, two lovers got engaged right in front of me... And I looked through the crowd that had gathered to see this gorgeous woman, all alone. My curiosity was piqued."

A tear rolled down Elise's cheek. Cindy had never heard this story of the engagement in Mackinaw City, the first sight Elise and Wayne had shared. It was a remarkable beginning—much better than a blind date at The Pink Pony (like her fresh start with Fred).

"Since then, Elise, we've built something together. We've grown and changed and learned about one another. You've learned that I'm a whole lot more annoying than my handsome looks should allow... And I've learned not to bother you in the mornings when you've set aside your writing time."

Elise snickered with laughter as her eyes glowed with tears.

"I'm rambling, now..." Wayne continued, wiping away a tear of his own. "With this silly ring and this cheesy speech, I want to ask you to marry me. Will you be my beautiful wife?"

Wayne lifted the top of the engagement box to reveal a beautiful vintage ring, a diamond-shaped stone that shimmered emerald green.

Cindy trained her eyes on Elise as Elise took in the first sight of the gorgeous piece. His hands dropped to either side of the box, cradling it.

"Yes. Of course, I'll marry you." Elise's hands shook so violently that they nearly dropped the velvet box to the ground.

Slowly, Wayne removed the ring from the box and slipped the ring over Elise's fourth finger. Through the quivering tension, Elise flung herself forward and into Wayne's arms. There was such safety between them. Such understanding. Cindy sipped more of her wine, her eyes growing foggy with a mix of love and sorrow.

Wayne hadn't proposed to Tara in front of anyone. They'd been out on his sailboat, watching the sun drop into the lake, casting everything in glorious oranges. *Did Wayne think of his first engagement, now in the midst of his second?*

Don't poison their happiness just because you're not happy, Cindy told herself.

Next came the vibrant celebration. Dean clapped Wayne across his back, reminding him of the time he'd said, "If only I had another daughter for you!" He hugged Elise joyously, grateful that the final piece of his family's puzzle would remain on the island for good. Tracey wept audibly as she hugged Elise, saying she would be "the most beautiful bride." And both Emma and Megan held one another, overwhelmed with emotion, and both probably imagining their own engagement. At twenty-one and twenty-two, they probably daydreamed about it frequently.

After several minutes, Wayne insisted that everyone sit down to eat the lasagna. "I'm just sorry I couldn't wait till after dinner," he explained. "But I thought I was going to pass out from fear."

"The great Wayne Tanton was really that afraid?" His sister, Sarah, tugged at his elbow, laughing.

"I'm not actually made of steel," Wayne confessed as he dropped into the chair beside Elise, who continued to admire her ring. "As much as I'd like to believe I am."

* * *

After dinner, Michael dinged his knife against his wine glass and insisted that he wanted to make a speech.

"I am your business partner, after all," he reminded Wayne as he stood. "I think I have a right to some words."

"Very well. The floor is yours," Wayne said as he draped his arm over Elise's shoulders. She cozied up to him, eyeing Michael as he took his stance a bit away from the table.

Michael resisted all eye contact with his mother and father throughout his speech.

"I just want to say that Wayne has been one of the most important figures of my life," Michael began. "Throughout my teenage years, I spent a whole lot of time in this house, learning from Wayne— how to talk to girls and how to hang a shelf and how to shoot hoops. After I had left for three years, I was terrified to come home because I wasn't sure what awaited me here. Thinking back, I shouldn't have been scared at all. Just as he always had before, Wayne picked up my busted self and put me to work at the coffee shop, where I had the opportunity to become a manager and now, essentially a partner."

Michael puffed out his cheeks, overwhelmed with the story.

"When I got back from my travels, I met Elise and just

knew that Wayne had found himself someone special. Imagine my surprise when I learned that Elise was my Aunt Elise. A happy coincidence? Or is it the stars up to their tricks again? I have no idea." Michael swallowed the lump in his throat. "All I can say right now, Wayne, is this. Nobody deserves happiness more than you. I hope to model the way you live your life in how I live mine, in love and in work and in my sense of humor. Here's to you."

Around the table, everyone lifted their glasses silently toward Wayne and Elise. Wayne turned his head to kiss Elise gently on the lips. To this, everyone roared with happiness and sipped their glasses, overwhelmed with the wave of joy that came with watching people you love have so much love for one another.

A little while later, Cindy stepped into the kitchen to grab another bottle of wine from the fridge, per Elise's request. She wavered slightly from her third glass, cursing herself, but then stopped short when she discovered none other than Michael stationed at the counter, his shoulders hunched as he read the back label of his craft beer.

Here they were, mother and son, together again.

"Michael..." Cindy began.

Michael cast her a sharp look. It seemed to demand, *What the heck do you want, Mom?*

"Michael, it was such a wonderful speech," Cindy breathed. "It was important for me to hear, I think. After everything with Tara."

Michael nodded pointedly and sipped his beer. He seemed unwilling to say anything else. Cindy had the craziest instinct to just start screaming and never stop.

"I just wish..." Cindy began instead, her voice wavering. "I wish you would tell me stuff. About your life. About Margot..."

Michael winced and glanced out the window. "I don't want to talk about Margot, Mom."

Cindy had the sudden sensation that she was speaking to a stranger. She reached for the bottle of wine in the fridge and slung it under her arm, heavy with self-hatred. Fred's animosity and cruel temper had created this crater between herself and her son. She wasn't sure she could ever bridge beyond it.

"Okay," Cindy whispered, turning back toward the dining area. "I won't bother you anymore."

She then made her way through the door and greeted Elise with a tremendous smile, one that felt forced on her lips.

"There she is," Cindy heard herself say. "The bride-to-be!"

When Cindy sat at the table beside Fred again, she shivered with sorrow and sipped her wine too quickly. Fred bent down to whisper in her ear, saying, "Are you about ready to go?" Disgruntled, he stood and headed for the coat rack by the door, hardly bothering to grunt a goodbye. This was the nature of things when Fred got into one of his moods. No time could be wasted. And she'd been on "Fred Time" for twenty-four years by then.

When would she have enough?

Chapter Six

During the first week of May, Elise's daughter, Penny, finished out her semester at Berkley and immediately took a flight out to the nearest Michigan airport to Mackinac. News of her visit traveled through the Swartz family, with both Emma and Megan growing dizzy with excitement for their "cool California cousin" to arrive— an actress studying at a prestigious university and living out their wildest dreams.

Cindy, Tracey, Megan, and Emma took an outdoor table at The Grind on that glorious May afternoon, sipping cappuccinos in the splendor of the sun as they waited for Elise and Penny to arrive.

"We have to ask her this time," Emma recited to Megan, wrapping her hands tightly around her mug. "We can't chicken out."

"I don't know. We barely know her. Why would she let us crash her place in Berkley?" Megan offered, scrunching her nose.

"I didn't know you two wanted to plan a trip out to California," Tracey said, tilting her head.

"Mom." Emma sighed, faking exasperation. "We were born and raised on this godforsaken rock in the middle of this huge lake. I think it's time for us to see something else."

"You can run as far as you want from this place," Tracey teased right back. "But you'll never find anywhere half as beautiful. Mark my words."

"Words, marked!" Emma's smile was all sunshine. She tipped her mug back to sip as a screech rang out from the street.

"Oh my gosh! Hello!" Penny, the source of the screech, rushed for their table, whipping off her sunglasses as she approached. "Look at the four of you! It's been too long." She bent to hug them, first her cousins, then Tracey, before ending with Cindy.

Why did she hug me last? Does she know that Michael hates me?

Elise looked straight from a magazine as she stepped up behind her daughter in a pair of boot-cut jeans, a light pink cardigan, and a little belt that highlighted her waistline.

"How did the pick-up go?" Tracey asked warmly, gesturing for Elise to sit in the free seat beside her.

"I think I sped the whole way there," Elise joked. "Only to arrive about thirty minutes too early."

"The plane can only go so fast," Penny teased, sitting between Elise and Cindy and crossing her thin, tanned legs primly.

Wayne appeared a split second later to place a kiss on Elise's cheek and greet Penny warmly. Yet again, Penny screeched with congratulations for Wayne, her soon-to-be stepdad.

"I just can't wait to help Mom plan everything. It's going to be the perfect wedding," Penny told them.

"Perfect isn't something we do around here. I'm more picturing a wedding that's a bit of a mess, with plenty of love and buckets of food," Wayne teased her.

"Maybe we can find a compromise," Penny said.

"Not that it'll be so easy to plan something, what with your mom's big schedule this summer," Wayne said proudly, eyeing Elise.

"Oh, she knows all about that," Elise affirmed.

"It's part of the reason I came back," Penny explained. "I have a small part in the movie!"

"You're kidding..." Emma and Megan said in unison, clearly impressed.

"I'm sure the movie will need tons of extras," Elise explained. "You can all be in it if you want to be."

Megan and Emma gave one another incredulous looks as though, finally, all their dreams were about to come true.

"That's right. The movie you wrote last year is filming on the island this summer," Cindy offered, trying to fill in the blanks for herself. She suddenly felt like an outsider in her own family.

Elise nodded. "They got it off the ground fast. I'm acting as script supervisor and producer and about fifteen other odd jobs."

"I guess that means it'll be one of the best movies ever made," Wayne insisted.

"Cheese alert," Penny said, jumping with laughter.

"Gosh, that reminds me," Elise began. "Tracey, I was just talking to a friend of mine in the film industry. She's head of costume design for the film this summer, and she was complaining that she really struggles to find anyone who knows their stuff in the fashion world."

Tracey's eyes shimmered with recognition. "Don't tell me you put in my name."

"I just mentioned that you're a truly fashionable, very in-the-know woman who just happens to already live on the island," Elise said with a shrug. "If she reaches out to you for an interview, don't be surprised."

Tracey yelped with excitement, drawing her hand over Emma's and squeezing so hard that Emma screeched, as well. Their table was like an exhibition at the zoo.

"This calls for a celebration," Wayne announced. "Can I get you ladies something to eat? Drink? I have a crate of delicious champagne in back."

"I think we'll need two bottles of that," Elise affirmed. "And a few snacks for the table. Croissants, a cheese plate..."

"I'll get all that started for you," Wayne said, just before dropping down to kiss her again.

Their love seemed to emanate from them. Cindy nearly allowed herself to smile but then remembered her own devastation, her own darkness.

How could she ever break free of it?

As they sipped champagne and nibbled at cheese, croissants, and crackers, Emma and Megan peppered Penny with questions about her university career out in Berkley. Tracey interjected several times to ask more questions about the potential costume gig for the upcoming film. Cindy heard herself say, "*Ahh,*" and "*Oh, that's nice,*" to several things that Penny and Elise answered, although afterward, she had no recollection of what they'd talked about.

After they finished up a lunch of quiche and salad, Tracey suggested that they all pop over to her boutique down the road, where she sold a collection of iconic dresses, blouses, slacks, unique jewelry, and hand-designed bags.

"I have a surprise," Tracey said mischievously.

"Uh oh," Elise said. "What have you got up your sleeves?"

"When Mom has that look, you know she's up to something," Emma offered.

On their trek to the boutique, Cindy walked alongside

Megan with her shoulders drooped forward. Megan laced her fingers with Cindy's and whispered, "Hey. Are you okay?"

Cindy nodded gently, her heart lifting with surprise that anyone had noticed her dark mood.

All I want is to be happy, light, and free, the way these women are.

Why is it so hard for me?

"I'm okay, honey. I didn't get much sleep last night, that's all," Cindy told her.

"Do you want me to walk you home?" Megan asked, furrowing her brow.

Downtown Mackinac was a cozy little ecosystem of cobblestoned roads and clacking horse-drawn carriages. Cindy paused as one carriage laced between her and Megan and the rest of the group. With this privacy, she turned her eyes toward Megan to say, "Your brother has broken my heart. I don't know if I'll ever manage to feel better again."

"He's still not talking to you?" Megan breathed.

Cindy shook her head. "Your father and Michael had that horrible brawl in January. Since then, I've felt like persona non grata. It's like he plans to just live out the rest of his life right in front of me on the island but keep me out of it as best as he can."

Megan exhaled all the air from her lungs. "He hates Dad. And..." She traced a dark strand behind her ear. "And he hates that you don't stand up to Dad."

"That's not fair—" Cindy began.

Megan gave Cindy a sharp look, one that read: *Let's not do this now.*

Did that mean that Megan was on Michael's side? Did it mean that she would eventually end her relationship with Cindy, as well? Cindy shivered with fear as Megan grabbed her hand again and tugged her across the street, where Elise, Tracey, Emma, and Penny waited for them.

Tracey had her key poised, explaining that she hadn't opened the shop that week due to "a large new shipment."

"And I just couldn't help myself," Tracey continued as she stepped through the door, which made the overhead bell jangle.

Cindy stepped in behind Elise, her eyes following hers across the shadows of the little boutique. There, in the back of the store, were five unique wedding gowns, in every shade of white, from cream to porcelain. Three of the gowns were vintage-inspired, while two others were sleek and sophisticated, similar to what Meghan Markle had worn when she'd married Prince Harry.

"Tracey..." Elise whispered, walking toward the gowns with her hands near her cheeks. "They're just... they're so perfect. I couldn't have picked more beautiful gowns if I'd scoured every boutique across Los Angeles."

Tracey beamed and admitted, "I've spent the better part of the past three weeks researching and emailing with fashion designers. They're all one-of-a-kind. And since so many couples get engaged on the island, the ones you don't pick will stay at the boutique for sale. Or, if you don't want any of them at all, that's fine. It's a win-win for me."

"Try one on, Mom!" Penny cried.

With Elise in the dressing room, the other Swartz women sat around the boutique, chatting amicably. Tracey stood nearest Cindy and leaned her head against Cindy's shoulder, whispering, "Remember when we went shopping for your dress, Cin?"

"It was the nineties," Cindy said, surprising herself with her sense of humor. "The styles were insane."

"I still remember the boutique we found yours in," Tracey offered. "That little place in East Lansing. The minute I saw it on the rack, I knew you'd go for it. Off the shoulder with sleeves. The skirt wasn't too dramatic, which I knew you'd like."

"It got me down the aisle, all right," Cindy agreed.

"Come on. You looked like a princess," Tracey told her. "And little Michael was so adorable in his little tux."

Cindy's heart ached at the memory. She gave Tracey a look, one that made Tracey snap her lips closed. Suddenly, from within the dressing room came Elise's wail.

"I can't get it buttoned all the way!"

Penny and Tracey hustled forward to help Elise get fully integrated into the vintage-feel gown, with a high neckline and tiny buttons all the way up the back. When she stepped out, fully buttoned, she lifted her chin and stretched back her shoulders, inspecting her image in the mirror. She looked regal and sure of herself, the sort of woman on the verge of building a brand-new life.

Cindy's stomach twisted with jealousy.

Why did Elise have all this bravery? Why didn't Cindy have it, too?

Later that evening, the Swartz women gathered at Tracey's place for dinner, wine, and conversation. After a full day of laughter and pushing herself to enjoy herself, Cindy found herself almost free and easy, conversing with Penny about her dating life at Berkley, laughing with Tracey about bad wedding dress fashions through the years, and nibbling little snacks that Tracey set out across the table. She thought twice about stories she wanted to tell about Wayne and Tara's wedding, then thought better of it, choosing to let the beauty of the present-day shine through.

You can't go back in time.

You can't live in the past.

Just be here.

"Have you talked at all about wedding dates?" Cindy asked a little while later, a pretzel stick lifted.

"Definitely after the film's over," Elise affirmed. "And once Wayne sees how insane I am during filming, he'll probably want to get out of the engagement altogether."

"No way," Emma said. "Wayne's so smitten. He doesn't know what to do with himself."

"You could burn his house down, and he'd still be like, 'Let's get married this weekend!'" Megan joked.

"Hey. Too close to home," Tracey pointed out.

"Gosh, I forgot about that!" Elise cried, rubbing her temples. "Everyone thought I'd burned down that inn to get money from your family. Our family, I mean."

"And now here you are, still taking advantage of our hospitality," Cindy teased, surprising herself.

Elise laughed good-naturedly. "I'll take as much TLC as I can get."

Around ten o'clock that evening, just as Cindy began to gather her things to prepare to leave, Elise received a phone call. She answered it joyously, which meant it was probably Wayne. After only a split second, her eyes glowed with sorrow, and her lips curved toward the ground.

"Oh my gosh," she breathed finally. "Are you okay?" Elise paused again, continuing to listen. Everyone in Tracey's home stood stock-still, waiting. "Okay. Yes, I'll let her know."

When Elise hung up the phone, she locked eyes with Cindy. Cindy's heart dropped into her belly.

"What happened?" Cindy's voice wavered with worry.

"Wayne was out with Michael, and they ran into Fred at The Pink Pony. Words were exchanged... And then, things got physical." Elise closed her eyes against the words. A tear rolled toward her cheek.

Cindy rushed toward her spring jacket, feeling on the brink of losing her mind. She hardly heard Elise's next words.

"They've been taken down to the police station," she explained. "Do you want someone to go with you?"

"Absolutely not," Cindy barked back, no longer as joyous and "light and free" as the others.

"Cindy, don't be stubborn," Tracey interjected. "You shouldn't have to go through this by yourself."

Cindy wanted to tell her that she'd been through everything else on her own— but it wasn't true, and Tracey knew it. Tracey had been by her side through all of it.

But this felt like too much to bear. Embarrassment made a bright red rash grow across Cindy's cheeks.

"Mom, I'm coming with you," Megan said, jumping toward the front door.

"Megan Clemmens, you are not going with me to the station," Cindy returned, furrowing her brow.

"Cindy, listen to yourself," Tracey began again.

But this was the last thing Cindy wanted.

She didn't want her beautiful, kind, and considerate daughter to see her volatile father and her brother, both bruised up from a physical fight.

That was the kind of thing you couldn't forget.

And she wanted Megan to be able to love them both, no matter what.

"I'm sure it's just a misunderstanding," she told Megan under her breath, not fully believing it. "Go home with Emma. I'll call you tonight."

Chapter Seven

Officer Ben Cutler stood in conversation with the front desk secretary at the downtown Mackinac Island police station. Ben was a family man, incredibly kind, with a propensity for gossip and eating enormous sandwiches with several types of meat. Cindy had known him for years and had recently watched him assist Elise with the ins and outs of her legal troubles with Alex, their brother, who'd tried to pin the blame of the fire on her.

Ben's kind eyes found hers across the desk. He broke conversation with the secretary immediately to step around the desk, wiping his fingers on a napkin that he immediately shoved into his pockets.

"Hi, Cindy..." He shook his head in disbelief as though the act of bringing Fred and Michael into the station that evening had destroyed him. He rubbed his fingers across the top of his skull.

He looked like he wanted to apologize. Cindy was grateful that he didn't.

"I came as soon as I could," Cindy told him.

"We're just filing a boat ton of paperwork," Ben told her. "It seems like no matter the crime, we're stuck with that."

Cindy nodded and buttoned and unbuttoned her spring jacket. The noise of the buttons popped in and out of her ear. "What's the bail situation?"

Ben wrapped his fingers around his collar and tugged. It looked like he needed to go up a size.

"If they were tourists, the bail for a fight like this would be around two thousand five hundred," he said sheepishly.

"Wow." Cindy had guessed somewhere in the ballpark of two hundred. Her guess had been off.

"But since they're local boys, I can let you off with eight hundred each," he said.

"Ben, you don't have to make an exception," Cindy murmured, barely trusting her own voice.

"I can't charge the full amount in clear conscience," Ben said simply. "And besides, everyone on the island knows..."

He trailed off as, behind him, the secretary cleared her throat.

"Yes, well..." Ben continued, running his fingers through his hair. "Why don't you take a seat in the waiting room? I'll let you know when we're ready."

Cindy walked like a zombie toward the attached waiting room, where several orange plastic chairs lined the walls. With her thumbs, Cindy pressed softly at her eyeballs until she saw orange spots.

Why. Why were they putting her through this?

The waiting room door creaked to a close. Cindy heaved a sigh and dropped her arms to her sides to find, to her immense surprise, a woman seated to the right of the waiting room. The woman wore a long flowing black dress, a thick puffy coat, and a big black winter hat. On the floor, her cowboy boots bounced around nervously.

Cindy's heart seized with the sudden picture.

This woman was Margot, Michael's ex-girlfriend.

"Margot..." Cindy let all the air out of her lungs as she took in this vision of a woman who was clearly frozen in the northern climate. "You're back..."

Margot's eyes were rimmed red with tears. With a pink handkerchief, she wiped away another run-away tear and then tried on a smile. Cindy rushed for the girl, overwhelmed with surprise and sorrow.

"Honey, it's okay," Cindy whispered, grateful to be able to comfort someone, anyone. It was her motherly instinct. "Were you there? When the fight happened?"

Margot puffed out her cheeks, then nodded. "It wasn't pretty." She hiccupped and dropped her eyes to the ground.

"When did you get back?" Cindy asked tentatively.

Margot just shook her head in response. Clearly, Michael had told her about his stance with his mother; the hatred extended beyond Fred and blanketed Cindy.

"God, I have to pee. Again." Margot sniffled and got to her feet, drawing a hand around an enormous stomach.

Cindy's jaw nearly dropped in surprise. Margot hobbled toward the bathroom door and disappeared behind, leaving Cindy to stir with wonder.

Margot was at least six months pregnant.

Clearly, the baby belonged to Michael.

Why else would Margot have come all the way back from Texas?"

But why now? And did the pregnancy have something to do with the fight between Michael and Fred?

With Margot in the bathroom, Cindy was left to her own devices. It wasn't so surprising that her thoughts turned toward those horrible months of her life when she'd been pregnant with Michael. People's eyes had followed her around, pitying her. *The poor dear. The baby will never know his father.*

Had Margot been all alone in Texas, weighing up the pros and cons of being a single mother?

Had Michael only just learned about the pregnancy?

Margot took a very long time in the bathroom. When she finished, she sat several chairs away from Cindy, indicating that she didn't want to speak. Cindy stared down at her knees, feeling crushed by the weight of the air in that room. Her grandchild grew in that woman's belly. *Would she ever know the baby?*

She imagined making a deal with them. *You don't have to have a relationship with me. But I will love that baby with everything I am. Please. Just let me.*

Officer Ben stepped out of the front area of the police station to greet Margot and Cindy. "The paperwork is complete. We can begin the bail-out process," he explained before turning his eyes toward Margot. They were heavy with doubt. "Margaret, did you say that you..."

"Yes, I can pay," Margot announced. "You said eight hundred?" She stood, then hobbled toward the officer before disappearing into the next room behind the slamming door.

Cindy stirred in her chair, feeling at a loss. She was reminded of all those years ago when she'd first dropped Michael off at kindergarten and watched him disappear behind the double-wide door. *There he goes. In a split second, he'll be grown up.*

Through the window of the separating door, Cindy watched as Officer Ben led her son out from the back cell. Michael bent to hug Margot gently, his cheeks blotchy from reckless emotion. Cindy told herself to shove open the door between the rooms and say hello, but she remained frozen.

When Margot and Michael disappeared into the chilly spring night, Officer Ben beckoned for Cindy to come to the front desk. There, she handed over her and Fred's debit card to pay the eight-hundred-dollar fee. Officer Ben then disappeared to retrieve Fred.

Cindy waited with her arms crossed tightly over her chest and her eyes to the far corner. She could feel the secretary analyzing her, perhaps trying to make sense of why this "well-dressed, upper-middle-class lady" was picking up a volatile man who'd been arrested after a bar fight. The pieces were difficult to put together.

A split second later, a drunken voice wailed from the far end of the hallway. Cindy stepped back in alarm as a violent-looking, red-faced man emerged, eyeing her like she was the devil himself. Officer Ben looked flabbergasted. He yanked at Fred's handcuffs and said, "If you can't control yourself, Fred..."

But already, Fred had begun to rip into Cindy.

"You damn—," he began. "Do you know what your son said to me this evening? Do you know what kind of disrespect I've lived with these past twenty-four years?"

"Fred, please. Calm down." Cindy hardly heard herself. She sounded so weak.

"I've had just about enough of both of you!" Fred howled back, his words inarticulate. He'd probably had somewhere in the ballpark of twelve drinks. He tried to yank his hands from the handcuffs, but they held fast.

Officer Cutler's yell was powerful, in total contrast to the softness of his heart.

"Now, Fred Clemmens! You are not to act like this in this station. Do you hear me?"

But Fred tugged harder at his handcuffs as Cindy sobbed gently in front of him.

"You blubbering idiot," Fred spat at her. "You were never strong enough to handle your life. You'd have been completely lost if it wasn't for me."

How did I ever fall in love with this man? Cindy thought then, remembering those long-lost days.

"Fred, that's enough," Officer Ben cried. He then tugged his handcuffs back as he demanded, "Dammit, you are going to sleep this off in the back room, Fred. I can't in good conscience let you go home with this wonderful woman."

Fred said several other expletives then, all of which Cindy heard clear as crystal. She stood, her vision shimmering from tears, and listened as Officer Ben locked her husband away in the drunk tank for the night. The bars clacked together ominously. It was a sound she would never forget.

When Officer Ben returned to the front desk, he furrowed his brow nervously and said, "Cindy... I'm so sorry about this."

Cindy leaped on his words immediately. "Don't you say sorry. This isn't about you."

"I just feel that..."

"Don't you feel anything," Cindy told him. "It'll all get cleared up in the morning."

There it was: her Midwestern practicality. It always came back through, even when she didn't fully believe in it. With Officer Ben, she felt foolish yet wanted to give him the idea that she knew what to do next. *She was a forty-seven-year-old woman, wasn't she? Didn't she have everything under control?*

"Do you need someone to take you home?" Officer Ben asked.

The idea of sitting in a carriage and being taken up to Pontiac Trail Head was torturous. Cindy shook her head violently.

"I'll just walk home, Ben. Thanks."

"He'll sober up and be able to explain himself in the morning," Officer Ben said.

"Yeah. Yeah." Cindy couldn't muster any other words. She wandered out of the station and into the darkness of the May night, yearning with all her might to run up to where Michael and Margot had disappeared, to hug them and plead with them to love her as much as she loved them.

Instead, Cindy walked through downtown alone with her hands shoved in her pockets. She realized she'd forgotten her phone at Tracey's but didn't feel up to picking it up just then. She couldn't answer all those questions or feel all those pitying eyes.

Yes, her life was a mess. She just needed everyone to leave her alone.

Outside The Pink Pony, Cindy paused for a long moment to watch the crowd. Since her first date with Fred, the interior had changed quite a bit, with several more televisions championing several more sporting events, a brand-new bar top and a smattering of extra tables. Marcy remained the bartender, although she was now somewhere in her mid-fifties or so.

If Cindy squinted just so, she could half-imagine a much younger version of herself and Fred in the far corner, having a beer on their first date. What had they said to one another? What had Fred told her that had made her think, *yes. You will care for us. You will love Michael and I the way we deserve?*

The house on Pontiac Trail Head always felt unnecessarily large. But that night, without the hum of Fred's television down the hall, it felt especially echoey and haunted, filled with the ghosts of the previous twenty-four years.

Still in the clothes she'd worn all day, Cindy crawled into bed and turned on the television, transporting herself to the world of a thirty-minute sitcom with a laugh track. Her stomach churned with sorrow. Everything about the bed smelled of Fred, of his cologne and his beer and his skincare regime. After two episodes of the sitcom, Cindy leaped up and tore the sheets from the bed, tossing them into the washing machine. She then lay on top of the duvet and watched as the fan spun slowly overhead, allowing her to drift off to sleep.

Chapter Eight

Cindy's sleep wasn't long-lasting. She awoke frigid with the red clock on the side table at 1:23 a.m. Groaning, she rolled over on her stomach, her skin itchy and her eyes dry, still with contacts plastered to them. Her head pounded, with the pressure swapping from ear to ear.

Water. You need water.

Cindy stepped out of bed, ramming her palm against her right ear and willing the pressure to cease. She removed her sweater, her bra, and her jeans and tugged on a big t-shirt, which read SPIN CLASS MACKINAC 2017. She then headed for the staircase, her tongue as parched as a cat's.

With each step-down, Cindy had to purposefully shove thoughts of her son and her husband deep into the back of her mind. *You just have to live through the night. Tomorrow is another day. Just get to the kitchen and drink some water. You can do it.*

But by the time she reached the landing, her cheeks were

streaked with tears all over again. She cursed herself, cursed her broken heart, then stomped toward the kitchen, flailing her arm around to reach the light switch.

When the light illuminated the living room and foyer, an animal-like groan roared out from the couch. Cindy stopped short, her eyes enormous as she forced herself to peer closer at the couch near the fireplace.

A figure lay on the couch, all wrapped up with blankets, her hair splayed out across her pillow.

"Tracey?" Cindy demanded, her voice high-pitched.

With another groan, the figure rolled over to peer out from the shadows of the far end of the living room. It was Tracey, her face scrunched and grumpy looking. After another moment of confusion, she snapped up, rubbing her temple with the flat of her palm.

"Cindy!"

Cindy staggered through the living room and eventually fell against the far end of the couch, where Tracey's feet were. Tracey scrambled up and wrapped her arms around Cindy, rubbing her back.

"When did you get here?" Cindy asked.

"Just a little while ago," Tracey told her. "I went upstairs and found you in your clothes on the bed."

"Not my best look."

"I couldn't decide if I should wake you up or not, so I came downstairs to decide. Then I accidentally fell asleep," Tracey explained. "So, I failed on all counts."

"Don't be silly. You didn't fail." Cindy swallowed the lump in her throat, then added, "It's so good to see you."

Tracey's arms wrapped tighter around her, cradling her. "I told you not to go there alone."

Together, they held the silence for a long time as, bit by bit, Cindy regained control over her breathing. On the table beside the couch, she spotted her phone, brought back from Tracey's house. Gosh, she was a good sister.

"Tell me what happened," Tracey insisted quietly.

"It's so embarrassing," Cindy whispered.

"Come on, Cindy. I could sit here and tell you four hundred other embarrassing stories from other islanders. We're all in each other's business all the time. This will be replaced with another story in a week or less," Tracey affirmed.

Slowly, Cindy explained to Tracey everything she'd concluded about Fred and Michael's Pink Pony brawl, finishing out with the surprise appearance of Margot at the police station.

"Pregnant?" Tracey demanded, aghast. "Are you serious?"

"It's insane," Cindy whispered. "My son is experiencing all these enormous life events..."

"Like punching his adoptive father at the local bar?" Tracey chimed in.

Cindy couldn't help herself. She laughed timidly before casting Tracey a dark look. "That wasn't funny."

"You laughed," Tracey reminded her.

"I'm exhausted. I could probably find anything funny right now," Cindy told her.

"At any rate..." Tracey offered, dropping her head back on the couch, "Michael and Margot are in the middle of a huge transition. They need you, whether they know it or not."

"I feel that way, too." Cindy whispered.

"But Fred continues to get in between you and Michael," Tracey said. "This fight..."

"Could be the final nail in the coffin," Cindy finished.

"I don't know," Tracey tried.

"It really could be. Margot literally waddled over to a different chair in the waiting room, so she didn't have to sit next to me," Cindy said. "And Fred..." She shook her head, remembering the red-cheeked man Officer Ben had dragged out from the back. "He hates me just as much as he hates Michael, now. I feel caught between all these different worlds."

Tracey rubbed Cindy's right shoulder distractedly, pushing a little too hard at times.

"I just feel like... I didn't push myself to figure things out," Cindy whispered, her voice cracking.

"What are you talking about?" Tracey demanded.

"When Jeremy died, and I had little Michael..." Cindy continued. "I just wanted to put a patch over my pain. I couldn't sit with it. I couldn't deal with it. And it's like, I just fell into Fred's arms because I never thought another person would accept me or accept Michael. And now look where that's gotten us."

"I think you're being too hard on yourself," Tracey pointed out. "Besides, you're forgetting those first few years. You and Fred were pretty happy. Always hanging out with Tara and Wayne. Taking Michael to the park and on hikes. Having Megan..."

Cindy sniffled. "I just wanted to pretend that everything was okay. Even when the cracks started to really form, I ignored them. And we never even told Michael the truth..."

Tracey dropped her chin to her chest. "Maybe it's finally time to tell him. Maybe that's the first step toward fixing the relationship."

"Won't he hate me even more for lying to him all these years?" Cindy whispered.

"If he doesn't find out from you, Fred might come out and tell him one day," Tracey murmured. "And I don't think you want Fred to be the one to tell him. Do you?"

Cindy continued to stare across the antique rug she'd placed in the center of the living room, decorated with an elaborate and old-fashioned floral design. Fred had always hated it.

"You're right, Tracey," Cindy whispered. "If only I wasn't such a wimp."

Tracey slung her arm over Cindy's shoulder. Her eyes were somber and shadowed. "We're all wimps, all the time. Haven't you figured that out by now?"

Chapter Nine

Around ten the following morning, there was a screech and then a slam from the door downstairs. Cindy and Tracey, both in pajamas on fresh, clean sheets in Cindy's bedroom, jumped awake and gaped at one another through the bright light of the spring morning.

"Fred?" Tracey whispered.

"I don't know who else it would be."

Cindy tip-toed to the doorway and listened through the hallway for the gruff steps of the large man. Sure enough, Fred stomped his way through the downstairs, finishing in his television room. A moment later, there came the purr of his television. She could practically feel him cracking open a beer.

A successful morning for Fred Clemmens.

Had Cindy said something to him about his stomping into the house, fresh off a destructive trip to the police station, Fred would have said something manipulative and cruel, probably about his earning the majority of the household funds at his dermatology clinic over the past twenty-four years. *Didn't I buy you this stupid house? Didn't I provide for you and your son?*

"Let him rot in that TV room," Tracey said, lifting from the bed and rubbing her eyes.

Cindy sat at the edge of the bed and thought about the next few days. It was Saturday, May 7th, which meant there was only about a month before the Lilac Festival, which she'd stupidly agreed to help with. *Should I drop out? Tell Ron that I have a family emergency?*

But when was the last time I did something only for myself?

"Why don't you come stay with me for a while," Tracey suggested, breaking the silence.

"I don't want to make everything worse," Cindy countered. "It's better if we just... pretend this never happened."

"Are you kidding?"

Cindy turned her head quickly so that a pain rocketed up and down the side of her neck.

"I mean, based on everything you told me last night, you don't want to forget this. You want to tell Michael the truth."

Cindy's heart thudded ominously. "I've never wanted to get divorced, Tracey. Maybe Fred and I weren't perfect for each other, but we've built a whole life together. I don't want one bad night to tear that apart."

Tracey glowered at her before nodding and sliding off the side of the bed. "You can do what you want."

"Thanks for the permission," Cindy barked back.

Tracey disappeared into the bathroom as Cindy curled up again in bed. With each pulse of her heart, her body seemed to shiver with sorrow. *You can fix this. You can figure out a way through. Divorce isn't the answer. Imagine it: the legal fees, the loneliness. Plus, you're forty-seven years old. Who would ever want to date you?*

You should have tried your hand at dating someone else when you were twenty-three.

At least you were still beautiful back then...

Her cell phone buzzed on the side table. A quick glance gave her a peculiar name:

RON WATERS

Cindy jumped for the phone and read his text.

RON: Hey Cindy! Long time, no see. I know we talked about you getting involved with the Lilac Festival. Are you still interested?

Cindy texted carefully with the tips of her fingers, nervous that she would make a mistake.

CINDY: Hi Ron! I would love to help in any way I can.

RON: Great. Would you like to meet this week sometime? I'd love to go over the details.

CINDY: Yes, please.

RON: How does lunch Tuesday sound?

When Tracey returned to the bedroom, she arched her eyebrow with surprise. "What's gotten into you?" She began to unbutton her pajamas, still committed to the way they'd been back in the old days— not caring about one another's privacy. It was a sister thing.

"Oh, nothing. I just said I'd help with the Lilac Festival."

"That's right!" Tracey said. "Gosh, you're so lame. Getting all excited about flowers."

Cindy stuck her tongue out as her lips twisted into a smile. "Just let me have one thing for myself."

* * *

Tuesday at lunchtime, Cindy reapplied her lipstick and watched the door expectantly, waiting for Ron's grand entrance. She'd been four minutes early and now sat overthinking everything, from her outfit to her decision to work for the Lilac Festival at all.

It had been a whirlwind of a spring.

Throughout the previous three days, she and Fred had tried to avoid one another like the plague, which wasn't entirely different than "ordinary" times. When she'd slipped out earlier that morning in a lavender dress and red lipstick, he'd stepped out of the at-home gym, slick with sweat and gleaming. Gosh, he was handsome. Cindy had made a point to walk right past him like she hardly saw him at all.

"Where are you going?" Fred had asked.

"Out."

"Okay. I have several appointments this afternoon and evening. I'll be home late."

Cindy hadn't answered him.

When Ron stepped through the door of the little vegetarian restaurant, he beamed at her. With their eyes locked, it was as though they were the only two creatures in the buzzing restaurant.

Or maybe it was all in Cindy's mind.

"Ron," she greeted him, extending an arm to shake his hand.

"Cindy. Good to see you." Ron sat across from her, hanging his coat along the back of his chair. "Still rather chilly out there, isn't it?"

"May in Michigan can be tricky," Cindy recited. "But the lilacs will be all right."

"You promise me?" He sounded flirtatious, lifting his menu so that only his eyes showed over the top.

After they ordered, Ron showed Cindy the smattering of events he had planned for the upcoming Lilac Festival, along with what would need to be done to prepare for them in the next month. Cindy took diligent notes, grateful to throw her mind into something that felt bigger than her and her stupid problems.

As they finished up their vegetarian sandwiches and their

freshly squeezed lemonade, Ron lifted a hand to alert the server that he wanted to pay.

"Oh, come on, Ron. We can split it," Cindy told him.

"Let me. You had to listen to me prattle on for nearly an hour."

"It's all about flowers," Cindy told him. "It makes my heart happy to hear it."

Initially, afterward, Cindy cursed herself for having said these words. But Ron seemed illuminated from them. He gave the server a twenty-five percent tip (which Cindy could only compare to Fred's usual twelve to fifteen percent) and then held the door open for Cindy, who basically floated out of it.

You have a husband. You aren't the type of woman to do this.

Oh, but it's so nice to pretend.

"Okay. Let's reconvene in about a week to discuss more logistics," Ron told her, setting a note in his calendar. "Lots to do. Lots to panic about."

"Let's promise not to panic," Cindy tried. "Let's just do everything right the first time."

"Easier said than done."

* * *

As Cindy wandered through downtown, light as air, she received a phone call from Megan.

"Mom. Where are you right now?" Her daughter sounded breathless.

"I'm downtown. Just walking around." *Daydreaming about a man who isn't your father.*

"Can you come to the fudge shop right this minute?"

"I'm seven minutes away."

Cindy kicked up to a run, hustling across the cobblestones and narrowly avoiding carriages. Only four minutes later, she flung herself into the fudge shop to find Emma and Megan in the throes of a celebration, playing music loudly, singing songs, and dancing in between large slabs of peanut butter and chocolate fudge.

"What's gotten into you two?" Cindy laughed outright, watching as Megan twirled around and around.

"You have to tell her!" Emma called.

Megan rushed around the front counter to fling her arms around her mother's neck. Her heartbeat was so frantic, like a rabbit's.

"Honey! What's going on?" Fresh off her lunch with Ron, Cindy felt like her insides matched her daughter's enthusiasm.

"I didn't tell you this, but a few months back, I applied to go to college," Megan said mischievously.

Cindy's jaw dropped. The previous year, Megan had first confessed to yearning for a career in the arts. Fred had obviously tried to push her away from these thoughts, as he felt they weren't "practical." Cindy was grateful his daughter had ignored him.

"And Michigan State just wrote me to say I was accepted!" Megan cried. "I can head to East Lansing this fall."

Wordless, Cindy dropped forward and wrapped her arms tightly around Megan, digging her chin into her daughter's shoulder. If only that digging in could keep her on the island a little bit longer. If only she could latch her daughter away from the rest of the world for good.

Megan talked to Penny too long. She learned to want something more than what we have here.

But that's okay, isn't it?

Didn't I raise her to be curious?

"I'm so proud of you, honey," Cindy whispered. "And so mad at you, all at once."

Megan laughed good-naturedly, stepping back to swipe the tears from the corners of her eyes.

Cindy puffed out her cheeks and added, "You were

always such a writer, Megan. Always writing little stories in your notebooks and little poems on the front pages of library books."

Emma giggled. "Can't you ever follow the rules?"

"I won't do that at Michigan State," Megan affirmed, rubbing her palms together.

"Your dad's going to kill you for going to State," Emma reminded her. "Since he's a U of M guy."

"Oh, Dad will be fine," Megan said, brushing the comment away easily. "He'll get over it. He'll have to."

A few minutes later, Emma excused herself to head upstairs to grab something from their apartment. This left Megan and Cindy alone for the first time since Cindy had run off to pick up Megan's brother and father from jail, one of the most dramatic moments of their family's life.

"I hope you're okay, Mom," Megan finally muttered, shoving her hands into her pockets. "I've been worried."

"You shouldn't worry about me," Cindy told her. "Just about yourself. I'll take care of everything else."

"That's not how this works," Megan reminded her. "We're in this life together, you know."

Cindy crossed and uncrossed her arms, suddenly heavy with the news she'd learned several nights before. After a long pause, she finally said, "Margot was at the station, waiting for Michael. She's..."

But when she lifted her eyes to Megan's, she recognized that Megan already knew. Megan's cheeks burned pink.

"I'm sorry," Megan whispered. "He didn't want me to tell you."

"Not a surprise," Cindy countered. "How long has she been back?"

"Maybe a week?" Megan tried. "It's been a whirlwind for Michael. He doesn't know what to do with himself or the state of their relationship or anything for that matter. I guess when he saw Dad at The Pink Pony, he found someone to take all his confusion out on."

"Did your dad say something about Margot's pregnancy?" Cindy whispered.

Megan wouldn't look Cindy in the eye. "You know how Dad can get. He's a bully."

Cindy's stomach twisted itself into knots. As she opened her mouth, preparing to say something, anything that might take the pain of this away, Emma appeared at the landing of the staircase, triumphantly telling Megan something she'd learned about a professor of Creative Writing at Michigan State.

A beaming Megan fell back into the glory of her recent accomplishment as Cindy sat stewing in confusion. The only member of her family who actually loved and cared for her would soon depart. What would she do, then? What would be left of her heart?

Chapter Ten

On an early-morning hike that Friday, Cindy caught sight of a creature up ahead on the trail. Golden coloring flashed quickly between the trees. Then came the jangling of a collar and the vibrant breaths of the dog itself. In a flash, her father's golden retriever, Diesel, appeared before her, leaping up to plant his paws across her chest adoringly. Surprised and lost in chaotic thoughts, Cindy screeched with a mix of pleasure and fear.

"What are you doing out here?" she cried, drawing her hands across Diesel's paws and gazing into his beautiful, shining eyes.

A whistle rang out from behind the curve in the trail. A moment later, Cindy's father appeared, trudging evenly along the trail as though he owned it (which, as the richest man on Mackinac Island, he basically did). Like always, he wore a dark red flannel and a pair of jeans, and his hiking boots dug into the soft soil of the trail.

"Cindy," he greeted her warmly. "What a surprise. You're the first person I've seen on the trail this morning."

Diesel dropped from her chest and circled her joyously, still panting.

"Just out for my morning mental health walk," Cindy offered. "The treadmill just doesn't cut it."

"You got that right. I need the trees, the air, the soil..." Dean said contemplatively, lifting his bearded chin to the light spring breeze. "There's nothing like the earth coming alive in the spring. That smell is so nourishing."

Silence stretched between them. Cindy realized she hadn't been alone with only her father in quite some time, perhaps six months or more. She felt she'd been hiding away from those she loved the most if only so she didn't have to acknowledge the weight of her own emotions.

"Did you hear about Megan?" Cindy finally asked, breaking through the quiet.

"She called me," Dean offered warmly. "Couldn't be prouder. She's always had a wicked creative streak, our Megan. She mentioned she was nervous about going to college as a twenty-two-year-old, but I told her it's all the better that way. She won't be as easily distracted."

"You have a point," Cindy murmured, furrowing her brow. "Although I hope she'll still make friends."

For Cindy, that was the most intimidating thing about life off the island. How did anyone create a social circle? She'd been born into hers.

"She'll be just fine," Dean affirmed. "Have you ever met anyone who didn't like our Megan?"

"You have a point." Cindy chuckled good-naturedly, surprised that she was able to smile. It felt good, opening her heart up on the trail with her father in the early morning.

"I was thinking of having a little impromptu family gathering tonight," Dean said. "We have a great deal to celebrate, what with Wayne and Elise's engagement, Tracey's involvement with Elise's film, and Megan's acceptance to Michigan State."

That, and Margot's pregnancy.

Did anyone else know about that?

"Well, I have no plans tonight," Cindy offered. "I can't speak for anyone else."

"I'll send out a message when I get home," Dean said. His eyes then scanned the space behind Elise, the trail he had yet to take. "Funny, we're going opposite directions. I'd invite you to keep going with me, but I have a hunch you're out here for a reason. A mental health walk requires solitude."

Cindy bowed her head. If only she could tell him about the innermost sorrows of her heart. If only saying them aloud meant understanding them.

"I'll see you tonight," Cindy said instead, placing a hand over Diesel's golden head and scratching the space behind his left ear. "Looking forward to it."

To Cindy's tremendous dismay, Michael and Margot declined Dean's invitation for dinner that night.

"That's the life of twenty-four-year-olds," Dean said as Cindy entered, waving his hand evenly. "It's Friday. They don't always want to hang out with us old fogeys."

Tracey stepped into the foyer to greet Cindy, raising a cocktail glass and showing her newly whitened teeth with a big smile. "Is Fred coming tonight?" she asked.

"He couldn't make it," Cindy told them, her voice wavering. In truth, she hadn't told Fred about the dinner at all, allowing him to waste away in that TV room watching the news from the outside world.

"That's too bad," Dean said flippantly, as though he didn't mean it.

Dean's housekeeper had set up the table on the enclosed porch attached to the back of the large house. Already, Alex, Megan, Emma, Elise, and Wayne sat around the table, laughing. A speaker in the corner played soft jazz tunes, songs Dean Swartz had loved his entire life. Megan jumped up to greet Cindy with a big hug, bringing with her a wave of new perfume. Cindy might have called the perfume "more grown-up," proof that Megan was ready to become the woman she was always meant to be.

"Penny is on her way," Elise informed them brightly. "She met some guy at the beach today and has spent the afternoon running around the island, getting in touch with her islander-side."

"The island has a way of bringing you into its magic..." Dean said from the doorway. "I still remember my first few weeks here. I knew pretty early on that I couldn't leave..."

"Listen to that, Meg," Emma teased. "You sure you want to run off and chase after your dreams?"

"It's only four years," Megan returned. "And then I can come back to the island and write the days away."

"Oh yeah. All those jobs are online these days," Elise pointed out. "You shouldn't have any trouble building a portfolio and getting clients. I can put you in touch with people in Los Angeles."

"I can't wait to brag about your success as a writer, Megs," Emma offered. "While I work the days away at the fudge shop..."

"You don't have to stay there, you know," Tracey pointed out. "Not that I'm asking you to leave the island."

"I have been looking at programs," Emma affirmed, her eyes trained to the ground. Emma and Tracey were thick as thieves. It would probably destroy Tracey if Emma took off elsewhere.

"Let's not get ahead of ourselves," Dean recited. "And at

least eat some dinner before we make any grand plans to escape Mackinac."

Immediately after Penny's arrival, dinner was served: roasted chicken, mashed potatoes, Brussels sprouts, with a dessert of raspberry cheesecake. Cindy found herself falling into conversation with Megan and Penny regarding things "not to forget" when moving to a university town. Penny had plenty of top tips for supplies, the best laptops of the current season, and how far away from campus to live to get the benefits of the college town and the campus at once.

"This is so helpful, Pen," Megan told her.

"The most important thing you have to remember is... whatever happens there, you will find a way to figure it out," Penny explained. "I think that's the biggest lesson I've had to learn in college. Being resourceful. Being on my own."

Cindy, who'd hardly ever spent a day alone in her life, stirred with fear at the idea. She remembered those months without Jeremy, growing baby Michael in her stomach. At least back then, Tara and Tracey had been continually by her side.

"How do you deal with the loneliness?" Cindy asked Penny, surprising herself.

Penny took the question seriously. The conversation died across the table in expectation of her answer.

"It gives me time to think about my life and what I really want it to be about," Penny said finally, her eyes flickering with emotion. "I think, without that time to process, I would feel a whole lot more lost."

Dean raised his wine glass. "I love listening to these young people talk about their perspectives. Reminds me of the heavy thought I gave to so many decisions I made in my life. I'm grateful for every single one of those thoughts. What's more, I feel honored to be related to such considerate and forward-thinking individuals." He gave Penny, Emma, and Megan a warm smile before lifting his glass higher. "Here's to the next generation. May you know that you have our blessing and our support."

* * *

A couple of hours later, the rest of the family gathered around Dean at the piano. This left only Elise and Cindy outside on the patio, enjoying the twinkling of the piano keys as the sound rolled through the open window. Before them, the leftover wine glasses caught the reflection of the moon.

Neither of them had said a word in over ten minutes when Cindy finally got up the nerve to ask the question that had been on her mind.

"Do you know about Michael and Margot?" Cindy couldn't lift her eyes from the white tablecloth, where someone had dripped a bit of red wine.

The fact that I have to ask my half-sister about my own son's child is heartbreaking.

Elise's answer was hardly a whisper. "I know about it, yes."

Cindy's shoulders dropped forward. "It hurts me so bad that he doesn't want me to know anything about his life."

"I can't even imagine what that must feel like," Elise whispered.

Just acknowledging those feelings in front of Elise lightened Cindy's load a bit. The clouds in Cindy's mind began to clear.

"I just feel so lonely in my life," Cindy breathed finally. "Here I am at a table with some of my nearest and dearest, and I feel like a stranger."

"You're not a stranger. We love you so much, Cindy." Elise crossed and uncrossed her legs anxiously. "But everyone can sense how unhappy you are. We all wish we could find a way to fix it."

"It's Fred, isn't it? Everyone knows how unhappy we are."

Elise held the silence for a long time. Inside the house, Dean switched the music from "*Under My Skin*" to "*Just the Way You Are.*"

"Last year, when I came out to Mackinac to look for a family I knew nothing about..." she began. "I felt like the craziest person on the planet. Alex only affirmed that."

"He can be difficult," Cindy offered, still protective of her younger brother.

"It's okay. Everyone can be. And I understand his instincts of wanting to protect Dad and his assets," Elise continued. "My point in this, though, is that pushing myself out of California, away from everything I ever knew, gave me more happy returns than I could have ever imagined."

Cindy blinked back tears. "What are you saying?"

"If you find it in yourself to take a leap out of your current situation... We're all here to help," Elise said, locking eyes with her. "You won't be out to sea without a lifeboat. We'll guide you through."

Chapter Eleven

Fred didn't have many friends on the island. One after another, they'd abandoned him, citing him as "cruel" or "manipulative" or any number of other words that Cindy might have also used. It was a surprise that when Cindy returned from dinner that night, she found Fred on the back porch with two buddies, Scott and Leonard, both of whom he'd gone to school with at U of M.

Cindy had met Scott and Leonard a few times over the years. They'd both attended the wedding, and they'd popped up for sailing trips and barbecues. Both were arrogant and jarring to speak with, hurling brags about themselves like lightning bolts. Like Fred, they both now neared their sixtieth year but hadn't slowed down yet. Leonard had only just married his third wife, while Scott played the field down in Lansing, mostly dating women thirty years his junior.

"Hi," Cindy greeted them from the doorway between the kitchen and the back porch, lifting a hand.

"There she is! Cindy-Loo-Hoo," Leonard called drunkenly. "We were just talking about you."

"Where you been, honey?" Fred asked, his voice edged with annoyance.

"Just down the road," Cindy answered.

Scott thrust a hand through the air and grabbed several Doritos from a big bowl in the center of the table. As he crunched on them, little flecks of orange flew across the table.

"Your husband here was just telling us about that son of yours," Scott said between chews.

"Just awful," Leonard agreed. "And after all you've done for him over the years."

Cindy eyed Fred as her nostrils flared. His eyes were half-open and shiny, proof that he'd probably drunk his way through seven or eight beers. Due to his intense skin regimen, he looked not a day over forty-three. He'd bragged more than once that he could get "much, much younger women" if he wanted to. He was probably right.

"I wouldn't have adopted anyone's son," Scott continued. "It's difficult to ever bridge the divide between a father and a son, anyway. When you take genetics out of the equation, it's basically impossible."

Leonard choked on a chip and whacked himself on the chest. Cindy remained in the doorway, seething. Fred gave her a half-smile, sensing her disdain.

"I haven't talked to you much since last week, Cin," Fred told her.

Cindy might have said something about the absolute idiocy of having to pick up your husband from the downtown jail—especially a man who was supposed to be a medical doctor and a pillar of their community.

But doing something like that in front of Scott and Leonard would have only aggravated the situation.

"I think you're right about what you said earlier, Fred," Scott continued as Leonard continued to choke. "Don't let him back in your house. If he disrespects you... your relationship is over. No matter what the legal papers say."

"Can you reverse adoption?" Leonard asked.

Fred took a long swig of beer. Cindy nearly vomited across the back porch.

"Fred? Can I speak to you for a moment?"

Both Leonard and Scott, drunk on their own seven or eight beers, imitated her after that. *"Fred? Can I speak to you for a moment?"* Their voices were high-pitched and silly, adding insult to an already very injured Cindy.

An injured Cindy who'd had more than enough.

Fred stomped into the house after her, throwing the porch door closed behind him. Cindy crossed her arms tightly over her chest and lifted her chin. Her heart felt terribly hollow, as though she'd never felt any love for him at all.

"I mean what I say, Cindy," Fred told her, towering over her. "That boy isn't welcome in this house. Not after last week."

Cindy had no real idea of what had happened the previous weekend at The Pink Pony. She couldn't know who had thrown the first punch or who had hurled the first insult.

All she knew right then was that Fred wasn't her first love.

He wasn't her forever love.

And right then, he was the boundary between Cindy and Michael.

As a mother, it was up to her to destroy that boundary.

As a mother, it was up to her to fight.

"Fred, I mean this with utmost certainty. If it's between you and Michael, I choose Michael every single day of the week."

Fred's eyes widened dangerously, lined with excitement. Gosh, he loved to fight. "Is that right?" He sounded so cruel, playing her like a cat with a mouse. "Tell me again, Cindy. Who bought this house for you and that snot-nosed kid of yours?"

Cindy set her jaw. She wouldn't fall into his trap. Not again.

"Goodbye, Fred," Cindy said firmly, dropping her hands to her hips. "This house means nothing to me with only you in it."

"You don't mean that," Fred shot back.

"Oh gosh, Fred. I can't even tell you how much I do mean it."

With that, Cindy turned on her heel and marched from the kitchen, resolute. Behind her, Fred howled with laughter, clearly not believing her. *Why would he?* She'd never stood for anything before. She'd only ever been the washed-up, sorrowful creature she'd been in the wake of Jeremy's accident.

But after twenty-five years, she was ready for a change.

She was ready to imagine what she could have been if Fred Clemmens had never walked into her life.

Upstairs, Cindy grabbed a suitcase from the back of her closet and filled it with essentials for the weeks ahead: jeans and sweaters and sweatshirts and underwear and bras and socks. She worked manically, never having packed for anything longer than a week somewhere else. When she went to the bathroom to grab her toiletries, she peered into the manic reflection of a woman she wasn't sure she understood yet.

Maybe soon, she would find a way to learn who she was.

Maybe this was the first step.

Before she headed out, Cindy scrambled through the back of the closet to find her old Canon camera, which she'd so often used during the nineties, back when she'd dreamed of being a photographer one day. After she stored the camera in one corner of the suitcase, she grabbed a box of film and several photo albums, which she hadn't looked through in over twenty-five years.

With each step from the second to the first floor, Cindy's suitcase gave out a wild *thwack.* Luckily, Fred, Leonard, and Scott were too busy being outrageous on the back porch to notice. Once outside, Cindy pulled her suitcase behind her, rolling it down the dark Pontiac Trail Head and back toward town. It would have been easier to just hightail it to the home where she'd grown up—but she needed to put more distance between herself and Fred.

Plus, she needed her sister.

Tracey opened the door after a second knock. She was dressed in a pink robe and a pair of house slippers and had recently poured oil and creams over her face, so much that she gleamed with the light from the outside lamp. Her eyes scanned from Cindy's blotchy face down to the suitcase she'd set on the porch with her and nodded with finality.

"You finally did it."

Inside, Cindy burrowed herself into a hug, closing her eyes as Tracey rolled her hand over her back. In the darkness, Tracey whispered, "Do you want to talk about it?" Cindy shook her head. *What could she possibly say that Tracey didn't already know? Wasn't it obvious why she would want to tear herself away from that horrible man?*

"Come on. You can stay in Emma's old room," Tracey murmured, guiding Cindy toward the back room that Emma had recently vacated when she'd gone downtown to live with Megan. "We'll be just like our girls. Roommates!"

Cindy laughed appreciatively, despite her eyes filling with tears. Laughter felt strange and jagged and unnatural. Maybe, though, it already had for a while.

Cindy changed into a big t-shirt and a pair of pajama pants and met Tracey in her kitchen, where she'd already brewed some hot cocoa.

"Can't believe you brought that suitcase all the way from Pontiac Trail Head by yourself," Tracey marveled.

"I'm going to have to get used to doing things by myself," Cindy told her.

Tracey nodded, her lips curving downward. "You're really serious about this, aren't you?"

"It's really over," Cindy whispered. "The fight with Michael was the last straw. It just took me a little while to fully come to terms with it."

"It makes sense," Tracey affirmed. "I can't pretend I know what this feels like."

Cindy shrugged. "It feels like dragging your body over hot coals."

Tracey let out a single laugh. "Sorry. It's just a perfect image."

"I know," Cindy told her. "And a correct one."

They shared the silence for a long moment as they sipped their hot cocoa. Cindy glanced down at the bit of dust that had collected in the kitchen corner. This wasn't anything Fred would have ever allowed. *Cleanliness is next to Godliness*, he'd said so often.

But a bit of dust had never hurt anyone.

Fred, on the other hand...

"Do you remember that I used to take photographs?" Cindy asked abruptly, surprising herself.

"Cindy, you were an incredible photographer," Tracey returned, furrowing her brow. "It broke mine and Mom's heart that you quit after Jeremy's accident."

Cindy stuck her tongue into the inside of her cheek. "I hardly even thought about it. It took every effort to take photographs of Michael, since it reminded me of the career path I'd lost."

Tracey heaved a sigh. Stuttering, she whispered, "Tara and I cursed ourselves for not pushing you harder to end things with Fred before they really got started."

"I'd already made up my mind to marry him before I even introduced you guys," Cindy told her. "There was no question in my mind that it was the right thing to do. Isn't that messed up?"

"No. It's not. You wanted to protect yourself. You wanted to make a family for Michael. It makes sense." Tracey added another marshmallow to her hot cocoa and watched it float around, bobbing in the dark liquid. "And it's not like Fred is some serial killer or something. I mean, it's messed up, but it happens. You can only stay with a man that treats you like dirt for so long."

Cindy laughed abruptly as Tracey smacked her hand over her lips.

"I'm sorry!" Tracey cried. "That was so inappropriate."

"But true," Cindy told her.

"You should take photographs again, Cindy," Tracey murmured. "If you feel called to do something like that again, then I think it's God telling you that your work isn't done."

"Or maybe it's my stupid mind trying to make sense of my life," Cindy returned.

Tracey shrugged. "I think that's about the same thing, isn't it? God works in mysterious ways."

Cindy rubbed her temple as she took in Tracey's words, knowing how correct they were. Tracey stretched her arms over her head as a yawn overtook her.

"You should get to bed," Cindy told her. "I feel guilty enough already for taking over your house."

"Nonsense," Tracey said, still mid-yawn. "It's not every day your sister leaves her evil husband. This night calls for long talks on the couch, at least one chick flick, maybe two, and plenty of snacks..." She turned toward the cabinet, searching through her bags of pretzels, peanuts, and snack-size chocolates, on a mission.

Cindy's heart ballooned. She rushed for Tracey, wrapping her arms around her and holding her tight. Tracey squealed and gestured up toward the snack selection, the likes of which Cindy and Fred would never have allowed in their home.

"Pick your poison, darling," Tracey teased. "Let's get this party started."

Chapter Twelve

On May 25th, the first lilac bush erupted in glorious lavenders, exuding that wonderful and nostalgic scent for all Mackinac Island passers-by. Cindy watched its blooming with rapt attention, knowing that this first bush meant that all others would follow suit. It was the first sign of the approaching summer, the first sign that all, very soon, would be well.

CINDY: Ron! The big lilac bush on Main Street bloomed!

CINDY: I think I might start crying. It's so beautiful.

Immediately after Cindy texted Ron, she blinked at the messages on her phone with sudden, rapt attention. *Had she just taken out her phone and spontaneously texted Ron Waters?* She hardly remembered having the urge to do that, let alone actually typing the words. *What was she thinking?*

She considered calling Megan and demanding if there was a way to "delete" messages before they were read by the receiver. Before she could make up her mind, however, Ron texted her back.

RON: I've been eyeing it on my walks. It's a sign, isn't it?

Cindy's eyes widened at the word "sign." *Wasn't this exactly what she'd thought?* She pressed her phone against her chest and lifted her chin toward the gorgeous lilac bush. The smell of the flowers seemed like a wall, eliminating any other sensations. She could have lived in this daydream forever.

Fortunately, she had work to do, and it all centered around the Lilac Festival. Based on her and Ron's recent meeting, she'd decided to take the social media matters into her own hands with a selection of photographs of the lilacs across Mackinac Island. Ron had seemed initially fearful of putting such responsibility on her shoulders, but she'd told him it would be okay. "I can handle it," she'd told him, without mentioning her photography background.

Because she was so accustomed to the old Canon, she had that strung over her neck as she wandered through town, snapping photographs of the newly bloomed lilacs. Megan had told her that they could develop the photographs and then scan them into a computer to be uploaded to social media. "I didn't know you liked taking pictures, Mom," Megan had said during this conversation. "That camera is really retro and cool."

Now, Megan knew one facet of Cindy's personality— her love of photography. Megan didn't yet know that Cindy was no longer living at the house on Pontiac Trail Head. Apparently, Megan had made a point not to talk to her father after the fight with Michael. This allowed Cindy to avoid the topic altogether for now.

Probably, it would all crash down on her head soon.

It didn't take Cindy long to get back into the swing of taking photographs. The light in late May was glorious, catching the healthy sheen of the horses as they clopped through town and the bright purple of the lilacs as they rose to the eggshell blue sky above. As she went, she also took photographs of tourists and locals, catching the "new energy" of Mackinac Island, which wasn't so different from the old. Maybe she just hadn't fully noticed it during her marriage to Fred.

She'd just been preoccupied for a few years, she guessed. Twenty-five, give or take.

There was a photography studio on Market Street, where Cindy booked herself a session in the dark room. The procedure in the dark room was incredibly delicate and all-encompassing. Cindy watched with bated breath as her film sprung to life in the liquid before she hung each photograph above and allowed them to dry. It captivated her, seeing the beautiful photographs form in a wealth of colors.

I still got it, she thought.

After she'd finished developing the photographs, she stopped by Ron's office to show them off. Ron's secretary waved her into his office, where he sat clicking a pen and poring over the Lilac Festival schedule, marking notes in a little notepad. Cindy cleared her throat to nab his attention. When he raised his head, a smile stretched from ear to ear.

"Well! Look what the cat dragged in."

Cindy laughed and perched at the edge of the chair across from him. "I hope you don't mind my coming in like this."

"No. It gets me out of my own head for a little while, which is always welcome," Ron told her. "What do you have there?"

Cindy opened the yellow envelope and tugged out her developed photographs, displaying them across the desk lovingly. Each felt so purposeful to her, a journey across the island and through her emotional mind. She hoped whoever saw them on social media felt that, too.

"My gosh..." Ron whispered, selecting a photograph of two elderly ladies helping each other across the road near a big, healthy lilac bush. "This has such character to it, Cindy. Really..."

Cindy's heart nearly burst.

"I mean, these seem too good for social media," Ron blabbered on. "It's like they belong in an exhibition or something."

"I hope you can still use them for social media?"

"What? Of course. Yes. I just feel so honored that you'd hand these over," Ron continued.

Cindy shrugged. "I'm just glad to be out there taking photographs again."

"Well, I'll get my secretary to put these online," Ron said. "If you head out and take more, maybe we can even feature them in the festival itself. We haven't officially decided on an artist for one of the gallery spaces, and I've been freaking out."

Cindy's lips formed an O of surprise. "An exhibition?" It was beyond her wildest dreams.

"I don't see why not," Ron told her. "Unless you're averse to the spotlight?"

Cindy shook her head wildly. "I just never imagined I'd ever have something like that."

Ron leaned back in his office chair, extending his fingers out behind the back of his head. "I guess you'd better dream bigger, then. There's no telling what you could do."

Cindy had never heard such words of encouragement.

Hot off the heels of this success, Cindy continued to wander through Mackinac Island, snapping portraits of sun-kissed tourists at Arch Rock, little squirrels and rabbits near Sugar Loaf, and sun-bathing old-timers at stone-lined beaches. A beautiful couple stood holding hands in front of the Grand Hotel, their eyes lifted toward a particularly enormous lilac bush— and the image was so good that already, Cindy imagined it being the advertisement for next year's Lilac Festival.

What would her life look like a year from then? It was difficult to imagine, especially so soon after her separation from Fred. There were so many stepping-stones between now and then. Tracey had told her to enjoy the here-and-now and not to press the fast-forward button too quickly. "These are the first days of the rest of your life. You'll remember them forever. Cherish them," she'd told Cindy.

A few days before the official start of the Lilac Festival, Cindy strapped her camera around her neck, locked up Tracey's house, and headed downtown with a mind to take more photographs and grab a light lunch. With a coffee in hand (purchased from another coffee shop, not The Grind, out of respect for Michael's space), she wandered, taking in the way the light shimmered across the old-world buildings and made it feel as though she'd stepped through time.

A genuine smile flickered across her lips as she walked. She felt delirious with hope.

When she spotted the young woman at the bench down the road in a pair of sunglasses and a white and red polka-dotted dress, she thought she'd never seen a more beautiful scene. The young woman was bent slightly to concentrate on the book she had opened before her; she looked captivated by the story.

Quickly, Cindy grabbed her camera, lifted it, set the shot, and snapped. Just for good measure, she took an additional one, knowing this would be one of her best of the year.

Cindy removed her camera from her face and peered again at the young woman, who'd just lifted her chin to look back at her. Her lips were parted with confusion, and her hair fluttered messily in the wind.

A split second later, Cindy's heart was laced with horror.

This was no stranger.

The woman on the bench was Margot, Michael's ex-girlfriend.

Cindy brought a hand to her lips, knowing how badly she'd just messed up. Margot closed her book and placed a hand over her pregnant belly. Apparently, the book and her posture had distracted Cindy from her stomach, but there it was, in full view: Cindy's grandchild.

Margot prepared to leave, tipping herself toward the edge of the bench. Cindy bolted forward, careful to keep her camera steady as she ran. "Margot! Please. Don't run away."

But women that far along in pregnancy weren't exactly quick. Cindy appeared in front of Margot even before she'd taken her second step forward.

Breathless, Cindy said again, "Please, Margot. Please, let me explain."

Margot placed a hand at the base of her back to steady herself. "You took my picture..."

"Yes. I did. But I didn't know it was you when I took it. I've been asked to take all these photographs for the Lilac Festival, and I saw you sitting there in the sun and thought, wow, what a beautiful photograph." Cindy spoke too quickly and probably sounded manic.

Margot removed her sunglasses just as she finished rolling her eyes. "Whatever. It's okay."

"Really, Margot. I wouldn't spy on you like that," Cindy told her. "I respect your and Michael's wishes not to speak to me."

Margot hesitated, winced, and then slowly lowered herself back onto the bench. "Sorry. I just need to take a quick breather."

"Of course." Cindy shifted her weight from foot to foot. "I remember being that far along. It starts to feel very, very real."

"You got that right." Margot seemed too tired to make a big fuss about Cindy's photograph. She waved a hand and added,

"The photo's fine. Really. If I look anything like a fat cow, though, I need you to never show it to me. Ever."

Cindy laughed, grateful that Margot had found a way to joke. She adored the girl's Texas twang, so different from her own Michigan accent.

Margot tilted her head, assessing Cindy as she slid her hand across her belly. The polka-dotted dress really did suit her.

"Are you surprised I'm still here?" Margot asked Cindy suddenly.

"I don't think so," Cindy offered, her voice soft. "You and Michael are about to have a baby. It's good that you're together."

Margot nodded, her eyes shadowed and sorrowful. "I hope you're right. When I found out I was pregnant, I had this whole idea that I could be a single mother in Texas. I'd raise my baby the way I wanted to raise her. She'd be only mine. But the reality kicked in a little while ago, and I just knew I had to tell Michael... and see what he said. It's not totally up to me, you know?"

Cindy's heart felt bruised. "All I can say is, raising my children was the greatest gift of my life. I'm sure you and Michael will feel the same. Especially because you have such a good partnership."

"Well, we're working on it," Margot joked as she slid a handkerchief across the back of her neck. After a long silence, she added, "I know how much you love Michael. He's stubborn. So stubborn. And he hates that you've stuck by Fred's side all these years."

Cindy closed her eyes against the weight of these words.

Cindy had a choice: she could tell Margot that she'd left Fred, or she could wait to tell Michael in person. It felt immoral to give such heavy news to this poor girl, who had enough on her plate as it was.

"You'll let me know if you really need something, won't you?" Cindy asked.

Margot nodded. "I will."

"You don't even have to tell Michael."

"I know. Thank you, Cindy. Really." Margot closed her eyes and heaved a sigh. "And again, that photograph..."

"There's no way you look like anything but a beautiful girl on a sunny afternoon," Cindy told her. "I promise you that."

Chapter Thirteen

Two days before the beginning of the Lilac Festival, Cindy and Megan stepped onboard the Mackinac Island ferry and headed for the mainland. With their hands extended over the railing, they peered down at the frothing water that rushed past the boat, warming their forearms beneath a bright June 1st sun. It had been a terribly long and gray winter, one of tumultuous clouds and volatile words from Fred and Michael. There on the ferry headed for Mackinaw City, Cindy could feel the passage of time pulling her away from all that darkness.

Once in Mackinaw City, Cindy and Megan strapped their backpacks to their backs and took a cab to the rental car place a little outside Mackinaw City, which was generally cheaper than the touristy places. Cindy had only ever rented a car for herself two or three times without Fred and found her voice wavering nervously as she asked the woman at the front desk what she wanted. *How silly I must sound,* Cindy thought as the woman placed her keys in her outstretched palm.

The rental car was a tan-colored medium-sized sedan with

automatic windows and a sunroof. Just after Cindy cranked the engine, Megan brought down all the windows and howled like a teenager on a road trip.

"That's right! We're gonna do this Thelma and Louise style!" Megan cried.

"Don't get ahead of yourself," Cindy teased. "Let's hope I still remember how to do this."

"If you'd sent me to Driver's Ed, I could help you out," Megan reminded her.

"I think it was you who didn't want to leave the island too long that summer," Cindy returned as she inched the sedan out of the parking lot. "I seem to remember some obsession you had with a boy named Cody Himes."

Megan's cheeks burned ladybug red. "Well, as my mother, I think you were legally required to knock some sense into me so that I learned how to drive."

"I didn't want you to go off and leave me for that long!" Cindy countered.

"Ah-ha! So, it was a selfish act," Megan pointed out. "Although I admit, I had a real thing for Cody that summer. Until he left me for Andrea, of course."

"Andrea. What happened to her?" Cindy asked.

"She's at U of M," Megan said with a sigh.

"Hence the reason you couldn't go there?"

"That's only fifty percent of the reason I didn't apply," Megan quipped.

The drive from Mackinaw City to East Lansing, Michigan, took approximately three and a half hours. For Cindy and Megan, who weren't accustomed to driving any distances whatsoever, the three and a half hours felt like a lifetime.

"I can't believe people do this all the time," Cindy moaned.

"Elise told me that in Los Angeles, people are stuck in traffic for hours at a time," Megan said. "Imagine being stuck in this prison, not moving, for hours."

"I would scream."

The real nightmare, of course, was finding a place to park in East Lansing that didn't cost an arm and a leg. Megan scoured the internet for "top parking tips" as Cindy traced block after block before finally landing on a parking garage that didn't seem outlandish.

"I really don't know how people live like this," Cindy growled as she shut the engine off in the dark shadows of the garage.

"Seriously," Megan agreed.

In the silence that followed, Cindy bit down on her lower lip with her teeth.

"What is it?" Megan sensed the shift of emotion in the car.

"I don't know. I realize that if you want to get around the next four years, you might really need a car." Cindy dropped her head back as disappointment wallowed in her gut. "I really did fail you."

"Come on, Mom. Didn't I tell you? I'm already signed up for Driver's Ed this autumn," Megan said with a wry smile. "I'm set to go."

Cindy's heart lurched with a million fears. It would take many lifetimes before she fully forgot that phone call she'd received from Wayne when he'd told her, *"It's Tara. A car accident. She's gone."*

"You just have to promise me you'll be careful." Cindy said the words before she'd fully realized she wanted to say them. She then dropped her gaze to her lap, cursing herself. They hadn't even gotten out of the sedan yet. They'd hardly even begun their trip.

"Mom, come on. It'll be fine. I promise you." Megan had all the light and freedom of being twenty-two and ready for the rest of her life. She shoved at the car door and sprung into the parking garage, which reeked of dank air and bad oil. "Let's go!"

* * *

The point of the trip to East Lansing, Megan's future home, was to tour the campus, sign up for her first semester of classes, and check out three apartment complexes that were appropriately near the campus without being too "freshman-heavy."

"It's so green," Cindy whispered as they walked along the edge of the beautiful campus, which was renowned for its old trees and lush, grassy grounds.

"Probably not during winter," Megan joked. "But I guess it won't be as cold as the island..."

"Nothing is," Cindy said with a laugh.

True to form, Megan was already prepared with her list of classes. Cindy sat off to the side as Megan greeted her semester advisor and discussed her plan for her Creative Writing major with a Literature minor.

"I'm twenty-two, so I'm a little behind," Megan confessed sheepishly.

"Nonsense," the advisor told her. "We have college students from all walks of life. Just this morning, I met with another woman in her forties, who's entering her first semester of college ever."

"Wow!" Cindy piped up from the corner, genuinely surprised. When both the advisor and Megan blinked at her curiously, Cindy drummed up the courage to say, "It's just that nobody ever told me you could just change your mind about your life in your forties. Maybe it's something I'm just now learning."

Megan's smile widened as the advisor tilted her head in confusion. Cindy felt half-foolish, half-grateful. Maybe that's how she'd always feel from here on out.

Megan signed up for six classes for her first semester: Creative Writing 101, The Art of the Story, 18th-Century Literature, Linguistics and the Origin of the English Language,

French 2, and a mathematics course that was required for graduation.

"Ugh, I hate math," Megan said, wrinkling her nose. "But you need either a math or a science, and I hate science more."

"Sometimes life is about the better of two evils," the advisor said.

After the appointment with the advisor, Megan and Cindy walked through campus again, headed toward the first of three apartment complexes. Cindy was thoughtful yet wordless, as though the quickness of her thoughts made her incapable of language. Megan spoke enough for the both of them, second-guessing a few of her course selections until she finally shrugged and said, "I can always drop something."

"That's the thing, I guess," Cindy told her daughter finally. "You can always change your mind. It's a beautiful thing."

The first apartment complex was, in a word, disgusting. Both Cindy and Megan stood in the center of the box-sized place with their noses wrinkled as the agent in charge of showing the place tried to explain why there was a stain the size of North Dakota in the center of the carpet. The countertops were heavy with scum, and there was a dank smell of beer in the bathroom.

"So, are you interested in signing?" the agent asked them.

"We'll see a few other places before we decide for sure," Cindy said. "But thank you a lot for your time."

"We'll let you know!" Megan called as they rushed out of there.

As they hustled toward the next apartment complex, Megan and Cindy walloped with laughter.

"We couldn't have gotten out of there faster if it had been on fire," Cindy cried.

"Did someone die in there? Is that the stain?" Megan asked.

"I just hope they're not all like that."

Once in the next complex, Cindy cursed her famous last words. This one seemed even worse, with a black mold climbing up the shower tiles and only a half-repaired hole in one of the walls.

"We would have this completely fixed by the time you got here in the fall," the agent told them.

"Of course," Megan and Cindy said in unison. "We understand."

When compared to the first two, the third complex was at least reasonable. It was quite small, with a bedroom that allowed for a double bed and a kitchen with a long counter beneath which you could place two stools. A window looked out across a nearby park and some giant oaks that seemed to come alive when the breeze cut through them.

"What's the rent?" Megan asked contemplatively, gazing out the window.

"It's eight hundred a month," the agent told them.

Megan hissed at the steepness of the price, even though they both knew that that was pretty standard when it came to one-bedrooms in the East Lansing area.

But given the horror of what they'd already seen, Megan turned on a heel, lifted her chin, and said, "Can I sign the lease today? I just want to get everything squared away before autumn."

Cindy's heart ballooned with pride. After years of being inarticulate about what Cindy wanted her life to be, it was a grand thing to see that her daughter was so sure of herself, so clear on her purpose.

"I wish I could bottle whatever it is you have," Cindy told her daughter a little while later after Megan and Cindy had signed the lease together (proof that Cindy had Megan's back if she couldn't pay the rent).

Megan's eyes shimmered with intrigue. "What do you mean?"

Cindy shrugged. "You're running after your dreams full speed ahead. I'm limping after what I want at one mile an hour."

"The photographs, Mom... They're gorgeous."

"They're a start," Cindy reminded her.

"Everything's always just a start until later," Megan offered.

After a long and heavy silence, Megan confessed to being "starving." "I think we should go to this burger place just off campus called Crunchy's. Apparently, it's legendary."

"Legendary burgers? Off Mackinac Island? I'd like to see them try," Cindy teased.

Crunchy's was the worst dive-bar Cindy had ever been in. College students had written whatever they'd wanted across the walls in many shades of marker, things like: TJ AND MONICA 4EVER and CALC 4 SUX. Cindy giggled as they slid into a booth that had been christened with the words PETER IS AN A-HOLE.

"I'd hate to be Peter," Cindy said.

"Nah, I'd hate to be whoever wrote that," Megan said, settling over her menu. "Peter sounds like the worst."

Cindy and Megan ordered cheeseburgers, fries, onion rings, and two glasses of wine. As they ate, the rest of the restaurant filled up with other East Lansing residents, with some students who'd stayed behind for the summer sprinkling in.

"I'm sure this place is totally packed during the school year," Megan said, her cheeseburger lifted and dripping its juices on the plate.

"Imagine. You might come on a date here or something!" Cindy said excitedly.

Megan laughed. "Come on. Don't marry me off just yet. I'm just now getting a handle on my career."

Cindy dunked an onion ring in some ketchup and tried to

keep all her anxious thoughts at bay. She was grateful that Megan had allowed her to help her on this journey. It was a big step.

"But you know that my end game is to grow old on Mackinac Island," Megan reminded her. "Have little babies and eat fudge and write books..."

"I know." Cindy waved a hand to and fro as she tried to keep her tears at bay. Overwhelmed, she took a long sip of wine and then, surprising herself, began to speak. "You know, I fell in love once. Really in love. On the island."

Megan shook her head so that her hair wavered violently around her ears. "What are you talking about?" She could probably already sense that this conversation had nothing to do with Fred.

The air between them shifted. Cindy swallowed the onion ring and then the lump in her throat, trying to drum up the courage to tell her daughter about the worst thing that had ever happened in her life. With watery eyes, she began.

"Jeremy was my high school sweetheart," she began. "We met when we were just kids and started dating when we were fourteen. Gosh, he was handsome, kind, loyal... Everything you'd imagine an island boy to be and more."

"Jeremy... Why have I never heard this name before!" Megan's whisper was raspy and filled with wonder.

"Your grandpa wasn't that happy about it, but I mostly moved in with him when I was twenty or so," Cindy continued. "He lived in an apartment not far from yours and Emma's. We had a lot of great times there, although they couldn't go too late. He always had to be up around four in the morning to go to work the freight liner."

"A freight guy! You were with a freight guy?"

"He looked great in that uniform," Cindy joked simply, unsure of what her daughter meant. Maybe she was just shocked at the contrast between Fred and Jeremy.

"Where did he go?" Megan demanded. "I mean, you lived together. That's big."

"It was big," Cindy said contemplatively. "But..."

How could she possibly tell her daughter this story? How could she open this wound?

"But what?" Megan asked.

"Do you remember when they reinstated the Mackinac Ice Bridge Race?" Cindy asked, her brow furrowed.

Megan's lips parted with surprise. "Yeah. I guess I was around twelve or so?"

"Around then. But did you ever hear the reason why they stopped doing the race before that?"

Megan's eyes grew milky with sorrow. "They said too many accidents."

"One in particular," Cindy murmured, training her eyes toward the French fries as they sweat across the white paper beneath them.

"Jeremy."

"Jeremy," Cindy repeated, forcing herself to lock eyes with her daughter.

Megan shook her head, incredulous. Someone in the back of the restaurant turned up the speaker overly loud so that the sound of some alt-rock band railed through their ears. It was the worst timing, almost laughable.

"I can't believe you never told us!" Megan shouted over the music. "I mean, God, Mom. That's big. That's really big."

Cindy wasn't sure what to say. She felt as though she'd just cut herself open and given her heart to her daughter to investigate.

"So, I guess you met Dad after that..." Megan began, still trying to add up the circumstances of her own life.

"Sometime after that, yeah." Cindy still wasn't eager to spill the beans on Michael's real parentage, especially not to Megan. It had to be Michael first.

Megan let a full beat pass before she finally spoke again, filling in more of the blanks.

"And Dad was never Jeremy."

Cindy closed her eyes, heavy with the weight of what this meant to both of them. "No. Dad was never Jeremy."

Megan slowly lifted her hand and draped it over her mother's as her eyes filled with tears. "I can't believe you've been carrying this alone all this time."

"It was an accident." Cindy's voice broke.

"I wish we would have known. I just thought..." Megan stuttered. "I thought you just..."

"You thought I what?"

"I thought being with Dad was what you'd always wanted," Megan continued, forcing herself ahead. "And in a weird way it makes me happy that you loved someone else. Someone who was good to you. Someone who wanted to make you happy. You always deserved someone like that."

Cindy gaped at her daughter, genuinely shocked at the generosity of her words. Any other daughter might have stood up for her father, at least the tiniest bit. But Megan saw the depths of despair in Cindy's eyes, and she insisted it was no longer something Cindy needed to carry.

"I guess this is as good a time as any to tell you that I've been staying at Tracey's," Cindy confessed. "I couldn't take it anymore. Not after what happened between your father and Michael."

Megan held the silence for a long time, even as her grip over Cindy's hand tightened. Together, as the alt-rock music continued to blare overhead, they contemplated what was next for their family.

"You need to tell Michael all this," Megan finally muttered between songs. "He really needs to know."

"I know that," Cindy rasped. "I just don't know if he ever wants to talk to me again."

Chapter Fourteen

The day before the Lilac Festival was set to begin, Cindy and Megan returned the rental sedan and wandered through Mackinaw City before dropping their backpacks at the ferry dock and waiting on the next boat. It was just past four-thirty, a clear and nourishing sixty-six degrees, and the crowd across the dock was pulsing and vibrant, filled with couples and groups of women who'd come from miles around to experience the splendor of the Lilac Festival.

A woman in front of Cindy in line for ferry tickets wore a t-shirt that read: LILAC FESTIVAL 1997. The ink of the shirt was worn-out and cracked, but the material remained a soft, beautiful lavender.

"Out of curiosity," Cindy interjected kindly, catching the woman's attention. "How many Lilac Festivals have you attended over the years?"

The woman's smile made the skin around her eyes crackle. "I've attended every year since 1991," she explained as she stepped forward in line. "I never miss a year. It's my dream to live on the island and watch the flowers bloom in real-time, but my grandchildren live down in Detroit. One week a year on the island is about as good as I can do."

Megan and Cindy smiled back at her as Cindy's heart swelled.

"And you? How many times have you gone?" the woman asked Cindy.

"We live on the island," Cindy offered, trying her very hardest not to sound like a braggart.

The woman's lips burst open in surprise. "You're kidding." She spoke as though she'd just met the Queen of England rather than just little old Cindy Swartz Clemmens. "Well, I'd have traded half my arm to have the life you've had."

Cindy laughed good-naturedly as the line tugged them further toward the ticket window. If only this woman could understand— life, no matter where you lived it, wasn't always a treasure.

But Mackinac Island was the only place Cindy could see herself living out her days. That was sure.

Once on board the ferry boat, Cindy and Megan sat on the top deck, where the wind rustled through their hair and threatened to take their sunglasses overboard. There was a soft ease between them, especially after their conversation about Jeremy. Cindy found herself marveling at the switch in their relationship. In only a few years, Megan had transitioned from a brace-faced teenager to young woman to one of Cindy's best friends.

When they got back to the island, Cindy and Megan headed straight for Tracey's place, where they discovered Emma and Tracey smack-dab in the middle of a margarita and nacho-chip fest. A speaker played Emma's newest favorites from a band called Greta Van Fleet, which sounded just like a modern-day Led Zeppelin to Cindy.

"Why can't they come up with their own sound?" Cindy asked as she sat around the porch table with the others, collecting a nacho chip and dunking it into some guacamole.

"Come on, Cindy. Let yourself really listen to it!" Tracey urged her. "It's not half-bad."

Tracey mixed Cindy and Megan margaritas as the old-world sound flew out from the speaker. With her eyes closed for a split second, Cindy could half-envision herself and Jeremy out on the lawn of the Grand Hotel, listening to Led Zeppelin and drinking domestic beer. These chords, these sounds: they reminded her of blissful summers.

As Tracey's spoon clunked through a glass, she asked Cindy and Megan about their trip to East Lansing. Megan spoke excitedly about the classes she'd signed up for, and the apartment they'd eventually decided upon.

"You're going to need help decorating the place," Emma told her mischievously.

"Uh oh. I have a feeling you're going to have a frequent visitor next year," Tracey teased. "I hope she lets you get your studying done."

Emma shook her head playfully as Megan tittered. "You know you're always welcome, Em. I'll be lost without you."

As Tracey passed the margarita across the table, she and Cindy locked eyes for a long moment. Beside them, their daughters chatted brightly about the approaching summer months and the denouement of autumn; they spoke about paint colors and bed comforter designs and the obvious choice between curtains and blinds. They could have been Cindy and Tracey during a much different year.

Cindy collapsed in Emma's bed at around nine-fifteen that night, a time that both Emma and Megan lovingly admitted was "geriatric." Cindy didn't care. She'd told Ron she would meet him at the Lilac Festival's main pavilion at seven-thirty the following morning, and she wanted to be bright-eyed and bushy-tailed, her eyeliner wings intact and her shade of lipstick perfect.

It would be her premiere as a "single woman" on Mackinac Island.

Not that she was putting herself "on the market" at all. Despite her little crush on Ron Waters, she'd been through way too much to just head out into the dating world. Life had chewed her up and spat her out, but she was in charge of her destiny now.

As she lay back in the darkness of Emma's bedroom, she raised her left hand over her head and slowly removed her wedding band and engagement ring, placing them on the bedside table with a clack. Her hand felt empty and oddly light, as though the weight of the rings had been much more than metaphorical.

The first day of the Lilac Festival was a flurry of activity. Dressed in a lavender dress (to suit the occasion), with a V-neck and a cinched waistline, her hair curled gently down her shoulders, Cindy darted around with endless excitement and energy, greeting island guests, leading tours of downtown, and giving at least two hundred people directions to their hotels. Occasionally, Cindy and Ron passed one another, both breathless and flashing enormous smiles.

"You good?" Cindy called out.

"Never better! Just can't slow down!" Ron hollered back.

That night, to kick off the Lilac Festival right, there was a "Wine and Sunset Boat Cruise," with tickets selling for fifty dollars a pop. Cindy was in charge of last-minute ticket sales and sat near the docks at a little table that fluttered with a lavender-colored tablecloth. The words "WINE" and "SUNSET" were irresistible for most Lilac Festival attendees, and the boat filled up quickly. The sounds of the boaters' laughter swelled across the harbor.

"All sold out!" Cindy announced to Ron when he appeared on the boardwalk.

"Nice work."

"They basically sold themselves," she told Ron sheepishly, unable to take credit for anything.

Ron's smile inched toward both ears. The breeze off the Straits of Mackinac fluttered his salt and pepper hair. Cindy dropped her eyes back to the lavender tablecloth, overwhelmed with emotion. There across the table was her now-bare left hand, its fourth finger bright against the sunlight.

"Why don't we take a ride tonight?" Ron suggested.

Cindy glanced back to spot the boat, where guests had begun to sit at little tables as well-dressed waiters walked amongst them, pouring wine into their glasses.

"Oh, I don't know," Cindy tried, although her heart burst with a resounding yes.

"Come on," Ron told her. "We've destroyed our bodies today. I think we deserve a little TLC."

"All right. If you're going to twist my arm about it," Cindy teased, leaping up from her chair to put the rest of the Lilac Festival pamphlets in her bag and fold up the tablecloth.

Once on the boat, Ron led her to the back corner, where a table had been reserved for the festival organizer.

"I had no idea I was here with a VIP," Cindy joked as she sat across from him. The wind caught her hair and slid some strands between her lips.

In a flash, a waiter appeared with two glasses and asked them their preference between red, white, and rosé. As the rosé floated into Cindy's glass, the sunlight caught the pink drink beautifully. Cindy grabbed her camera from her bag and snapped a photograph of the glass and the water and, naturally, Ron, who sat directly beside it.

"I didn't realize I'd be the subject of your next round of

photography," Ron said, both embarrassed and pleased. The tops of his cheeks burned red.

"The festival organizer should be the star of every photograph," Cindy teased.

"I don't know if I have the face for that," Ron quipped.

Beneath them, the motor of the ferry roared open as the boat operators unattached the ropes that tied them to the dock. There was a moment of hesitation as every member on board glanced out toward the orange horizon line, captivated with the orb of the sun.

"It's funny," Cindy murmured after a moment. "The sun sets every single day, but we always find a way to be captivated by it."

"It never sets the same way twice," Ron said.

As the ferry continued across the Straits of Mackinac, a jazz quintet of alto sax, an electric keyboard, a small drum set, a double bass, and a trumpet began to play on the top deck. The music was soulful and alive and seemed to draw Cindy's heart up from her stomach to her throat.

Is this really happening? Is this really my life?

"Shoot." Ron glanced at his phone, furrowing his brow at a recent message.

"What's up?"

"Ah, nothing."

"Is it something to do with the festival?"

Ron grimaced. "The woman who'd agreed to host the lilac-planting seminars over the next week got sick on the way up here from Grand Rapids. I'd hate to cancel those sessions."

"Oh!" Cindy splayed a hand over her chest warmly. "I don't mind doing something like that."

"You'd teach the seminars?" he asked.

"Of course. You know how much I love gardening. My mother always said I had a green thumb. I'd love to pass along that knowledge to people."

Ron beamed and took a long sip of his Bordeaux. "You've been a Godsend, Cindy. I can't tell you how many times you've saved my rear this month."

"It's been my pleasure. Really." Cindy was surprised and initially embarrassed at how genuine she sounded. She took a long sip of her wine, closing her eyes as the dry and slightly sweet taste filtered across her tongue.

"Can I ask you a question?"

Cindy nodded, praying that it wouldn't be about her lack of a wedding ring. She wasn't ready to discuss that.

"Why didn't you volunteer for the Lilac Festival before this year?" Ron continued. "I mean, you're such a natural at it. And you have a real love for the festival, more so than most other islanders."

Cindy held her wine glass with dainty fingers, watching as the bass player thumped his way across the thick strings of his instrument. All the while, Ron remained captivated by her.

"To be honest..." Cindy began finally, pushing herself just as she had in East Lansing with her daughter. "I was very occupied the past twenty-four years. I had very little time for myself or my hobbies. I think I almost lost myself."

"You have children, don't you?" Ron tried.

"I do."

Ron's eyes grew shadowed. "It can happen. Women take on the housework and the childcare and odds and ends of family life. When do you have the time for yourself? I regret to confess that I probably allowed that to happen within my own marriage." Ron's eyes dropped toward his hands, which sat sadly across the table.

He, too, had removed his wedding ring.

But Cindy didn't have any other context to know what had happened to him or his marriage. Ron wasn't an islander, and he obviously didn't communicate his past traumas to other islanders. Otherwise, Cindy would have heard the gossip by then.

"I'm sure whatever happened, she's grateful for every moment she spent with your children anyway," Cindy offered softly, unsure of what to say.

Ron nodded, giving her a tender smile. After a long and difficult swallow, he said, "And I'm sure your children are happy that you're right here, now. Going after your dreams."

Chapter Fifteen

The sunset boat tour finished at ten o'clock that night. Ron Waters watched from the top deck as the ferry boat workers hustled off the little ramp, tying intricate knots as the boat stabilized against the docks. Beside him, Cindy Swartz Clemmens sipped the last of her third glass of rosé, her eyes glossy after their two-hour flirtatious conversation. There was no way, yet, to know if the conversation had meant anything at all. Behind them, the jazz quintet finished out their final number with a collective and somber sigh.

It had been a beautiful night, but it was time to close the shop and go home.

Ron and Cindy waited on the far end of the docks to say goodnight to the sunset boat tour attendees, all of whom seemed to float toward their hotels, giddy from fatigue and too much wine. At one point, Cindy lifted a hand to wave goodbye to a younger couple and accidentally slipped her hand against his. Ron shivered with longing but soon shoved the thought as far back into the hallways of his mind as he could.

Only days ago, when he'd seen her last, she'd been wearing a wedding ring. Just because she'd removed it, didn't mean her marriage was really and truly over. It just meant she was having doubts. Ron had seen this a number of times, including with a woman he'd dated briefly down in Lansing two years before. After four or five dates of "just getting to know one another," she'd gone back to her husband. Que séra, séra.

"I'd better head home," Cindy told him sleepily as the last of the cast members departed. "I have that lilac-planting seminar bright and early tomorrow. Don't want to be late."

"Thanks again for taking that over. You can find all the supplies for the seminars in the back of my office. Here." Ron brandished his office key and passed it over to her. The sharp edges caught the moonlight.

"Are you sure?" Cindy asked, taking his key hesitantly.

"What are you going to do? Run off with twenty-five pounds of soil?" Ron joked.

Cindy blushed awkwardly, pocketing the key. "I appreciate it. But I'll see you around tomorrow afternoon?"

"I'll be around."

Cindy and Ron parted ways a few minutes later, with Cindy ducking up Market Street and Ron lingering back on Main. With his hands shoved in his pockets, he lifted his chin toward that moon, which seemed heavier than normal and creamy against the dark night. The Pink Pony bar roared with activity a block away, and, faced with the next few somber hours at home alone, he skirted toward the noise, ready for a nightcap.

Although Ron didn't have many friends on Mackinac Island, everyone inside The Pink Pony greeted him by name. That's what you got when you organized the Lilac Festival for ten years in a row. Marcy, the bartender, brought a stool out for him from the back to fit him into the side of the bar, which offered a decent view of the basketball game on the television that hung above.

"How was the first day of the festival?" Marcy asked as she poured him a pint.

"A roaring success," Ron reported, laughing at himself.

"The bar is obviously packed with lilac lovers," Marcy teased. "Thanks for the business."

"I didn't invent the Lilac Festival," Ron returned. "I just keep it going, year after year."

"Someone's gotta do it," Marcy said before speeding off to help a table in the back.

Ron nursed his beer, his feet propped up on the base of his stool. Around him, the revelers told loud stories about past eras, the "golden years" of their lives. An older couple in the corner held hands over the table, grinning sheepishly at one another as their wedding bands glinted in the soft light. Ron took a long drink of beer, coating his tongue.

That should be Rose and I.

It was always supposed to be Rose and I.

The thought smacked him over the skull, stopping him in his tracks. He hated when thoughts like that cropped up, as they made him unappreciative for the life he'd built himself since Rose's death. That said, maybe it was natural, especially since so many of the things Ron had done since then had been "for" Rose, in a way. She'd always longed to live on Mackinac Island, especially during the Lilac Festival, which she'd forced him to attend year after year until her death twelve years before. Two years after that, Ron had read about an opening on the island for Lilac Festival Organizer. He'd watched himself dial the number listed in the article and listened to himself describe his "organizational capabilities and his love of lilacs." He wasn't ever sure what the afterlife was all about, but he wouldn't have been surprised to learn that Rose had worked through him that day, forcing him to make that call and set up the next phase of his life.

Now that he was retired from his career in accounting down in Lansing, he'd even half-considered moving to the island full-time. But that sort of move required the social skills he wasn't sure he had. Still, with both of his children living outside of Michigan, he was faced with a terrifying question: *what came next*?

Three seats down the bar sat the owner of The Grind, Wayne Tanton. When the two seats between them cleared out, Wayne lifted his beer in greeting as he said, "You must be tired. The festival always takes it out of me. Can't imagine what it means to organize it."

Ron laughed good-naturedly, grateful to bemoan the exhaustion of the day with an islander. "The Grind picked up a lot of traffic today?"

Wayne slid a hand across his forehead, exasperated. "We had a rush of folks that lasted between eleven in the morning and four-thirty in the afternoon. Every table in the place was full. We ran out of everything, and two of our busboys threatened to quit."

"No!"

Wayne shook his head. "I think they were just kidding. I gave them free cookies and sent them back out there, telling them hard work builds character. My business partner, Michael, is still there now, finishing up inventory to see what we need to order. He's supposed to meet me here for a beer."

Above them on the television, a basketball player charged down the court before pounding the ball just above the hoop, narrowly missing the points. Wayne hissed with one eye on the TV.

"Their heads are out of the game tonight," Wayne reported.

"No doubt," Ron heard himself say, although he hadn't

been paying much attention at all. *This was the way you communicated at bars, wasn't it? Maybe this was proof that his social skills were better than he thought?*

Wayne and Ron stared up at the screen until the commercial break as their beers sweated against the humidity of the bar. At the commercial break, Wayne slid down the bar to take the chair directly next to Ron. With a shrug, he said, "Poor Michael. I have a hunch he'll be stuck at the coffee shop longer than both of us thought."

After another drink, Wayne tilted his head toward Ron and said, "Rumor has it you're one of the first male Lilac Festival organizers we've had on the island in many years. I must admit that I don't care much about flowers. Aesthetics were never my strong suit. What brought you into the business?"

Ron's genuine shock at the question played out across his face. Wayne reflected his expression and hurriedly said, "I don't mean to pry. If flowers are your thing..."

"It's not that I don't like flowers," Ron said finally, laughing at himself and the situation. "I just... well. To be honest with you, the Lilac Festival was my wife's favorite event of the year. She counted down the days until we took off for Mackinac Island every June. She even got obsessive about it, making sure that we stayed in the same hotel room year after year."

Wayne's eyes became faraway with the mention of Ron's wife in the past tense. Ron's tongue felt thick as sandpaper. Maybe he'd already shared too much.

"I don't know if anyone's told you this, Ron, but I'm a widower, myself," Wayne revealed, his voice hardly loud enough to cut through the chaotic sounds of the bar.

Ron's heart grew softer at the edges. It was a rare thing to meet someone who shared a similar loss. It was as though they'd walked the same dark path.

"Nobody told me," Ron managed to say.

"Car accident. For a long time, I thought I might just leave the island, you know? Too painful to be here in the midst of all these memories. But after a while, I realized that the memories were good, in a way. I don't want to throw them all away. She was such a huge part of my life. We were inextricably linked. And now that I'm writing a new chapter..." Wayne stalled for a moment as his eyes glowed with tears. "I feel her blessing here."

Ron nodded, thinking again of Cindy's generous smile and the way the orange sunset caught the curls of her hair. He thought again of her finger, gently fluttering against his hand when she'd lifted it to wave to the boat tour attendees.

He also thought of Rose's laughter, twinkling out across the cobblestone streets as they danced through town, hand-in-hand. Those times would always live inside his heart. But would he remain locked inside his heart, unwilling to feel new feelings—unwilling to see new sights?

"You said you're writing a new chapter?" Ron asked.

Wayne nodded as his lips curved youthfully into a smile. "I just got engaged, if you can believe it."

"Congratulations. Who's the lucky woman?"

"She's a newbie on the island," Wayne continued. "She came last autumn hunting around for her birth father and made a big mess of things. Everything worked out in the end, though. Certainly for me and Elise, anyway."

"Wow. Nobody told me what kind of drama I miss when I leave the island at the start of every autumn," Ron joked.

"That's right. Maybe you should stick around for an entire chilly season or two and see what happens," Wayne said.

"Maybe I will." Ron lifted his eyes back to the basketball game to watch as the same forward from the previous missed shot flung the ball through the air, nabbing three points.

"Yes!" Wayne cried, pounding his fist against the bar.

"That's enough out of you," Marcy teased. "You think I'm running a college bar in here?"

"Sorry, Miss Marcy," Wayne apologized.

Marcy rolled her eyes toward Ron as if to say: see what I have to deal with?

"I have to admit, you islanders are something else," Ron continued when the commercials jangled back on the television. "I've never met people more genuine and interesting and willing to laugh in my life. Like, this woman who's been helping me with the Lilac Festival? I don't think I've ever met anyone like her before. We just chatted through the entire sunset boat tour."

Wayne's eyes glittered with intrigue. "Who are you talking about? Sounds like juicy gossip to me."

"No, no. I mean, I don't think so." Ron waved a hand in front of his face, recognizing he'd gone too far. "It's not like we're anything to each other. She just showed me such joy and empathy tonight. And sometimes, this weary old heart doesn't know what to do with that."

"Come on, Ron. Who've you got a crush on?"

"It's no crush! I told you. I'm a fifty-one-year-old man."

Wayne, exasperated, glanced Marcy's way and said, "Marcy, you know everything. Who's helping Ron out at the Lilac Festival?"

"It's Cindy Swartz if you must know," Marcy tossed back. "But I don't want to get involved with any gossip."

Wayne's lips parted with genuine surprise. Slowly, he inched his eyes back toward Ron, who sat in stunned silence at the mention of Cindy's name.

"Cindy Swartz, huh?" Wayne repeated.

"I guess as an islander, you must know her well."

"Better than well, I reckon," Wayne returned.

Ron's heart started to beat at a rabbit's pace. He sipped his beer, his stomach swirling with anxiety.

"My wife and Cindy were best of friends," Wayne continued. "But the Cindy I've known the past twenty or so years... isn't anything the way you describe her."

Ron tilted his head, intrigued. "What do you mean?"

"There's always been a darkness to Cindy," Wayne continued. "Especially over the past few years, it was difficult to get her to laugh or smile or tell a story. I love her a lot. She's like a sister. But I never in a million years would have guessed that the woman you're speaking of is Cindy."

Together, the two men shared the silence, punctuated only by the commercials on the televisions and the laughter around the bar. Ron sipped his drink, wondering yet again about the loss of Cindy's wedding ring and whether it meant anything at all.

"Well, in any case," Wayne continued. "I'm just glad she has a friend in you. Between her monstrous husband, her frayed relationship with her son, the death of her best friend, and now her daughter headed off the college, I think she needs one more than ever. I'm glad you brought such light into her life. Even if it was with flowers, which I'll never understand at all."

Ron laughed good-naturedly. He eyed Marcy again, who seemed to pretend to be in the midst of counting out five-dollar bills. You could practically see her ears sharpening to hear the words between the two men, her source of gossip for the evening.

"All right, Marcy. You can stop eavesdropping on us and get us another round on me," Wayne told her.

"What makes you think that either of you has anything interesting to say at all?" Marcy joked as she reached for two clean pint glasses. "I've got problems of my own, you know. My life doesn't revolve around you."

"Quit lying to yourself, Marcy," Wayne continued as he finished up the froth in his pint. "I know you thrive off gossip. The entire island does."

Ron fell into the bouncing conversation between Wayne and Marcy, grateful to put his mind elsewhere. After he finished his second drink, he over-tipped Marcy and shook Wayne's hand goodnight. Overwhelmed with emotion, he hardly managed more than a brief, "Thank you." He hoped Wayne understood what he meant.

Chapter Sixteen

Cindy had added Ron's office key to her keychain. It felt like a symbol, linking him to her separate world of house keys and mailbox keys and keys to Tracey's back garden shed. Outside of Ron's office at the ridiculous hour of six-thirty the following morning, a shiver ran up and down her spine as she slid his key into the lock and turned, stepping into a world of someone else's design— the rented office space that Ron called "home" during the months leading up to the Lilac Festival.

Just as Ron had told her, the lilac-planting seminar's tools were located in the back corner of his office. A wheelbarrow leaned against the wall, carrying several bags of soil, lilac bulbs, and a watering can. A prepared speech had been printed out with talking points for the previous lilac-planting seminar teacher, but after an initial read-through, Cindy deemed the print-out too sterile. As a seasoned gardener, she had lilac planting down pat; as an islander, she wanted to add spice and flair to her lesson, telling little stories about her time on the island, previous Lilac Festivals, and why lilacs grew so well on the island during June.

At eight-thirty sharp, a bright-eyed Cindy greeted seven new lilac students, women, and men between the ages of thirty-five and eighty-five who'd come from as far away as Bangor, Maine and as close as Mackinaw City.

To begin the lesson, Cindy explained the history of Mackinac Island lilacs.

"The lilacs that you see growing across the island are the very same lilacs that grew here more than two hundred years ago. That might come as a surprise to many of you, as lilacs aren't native to the United States. Hundreds of years ago, lilacs were brought over by Dutch and French immigrants, and then eventually, as settlers continued west, lilacs were brought here to the island. It's said that the Hubbard family was the first to plant a lilac on the island, although there's a journal entry from Thoreau that cites lilacs in bloom here on the island as early as 1861."

The seven students at the lilac planting seminar remained captivated throughout Cindy's story, frequently asking questions and tilting their heads with wonder. Cindy continued to tell them that the festival itself had begun in the year 1948 as an attempt to mimic the joy and celebration of the Washington DC cherry blossom festival. "Of course, Mackinac's Lilac Festival is a joy all its own, now," she continued. "With a heart all its own."

After instructing her students on lilac planting, Cindy stood with soiled palms, swiped the back of her hand across her forehead, and caught sight of Ron Waters across the street, watching her. Her heart skipped a beat. Her students, all up to their elbows in soil, chatted amicably beneath the glorious spring sun.

Cindy practically skipped toward Ron, feeling light as air.

Ron's eyes shimmered as she approached. There was no doubt in her mind: he was pleased to see her.

"How did your first seminar go?" he asked.

"Oh gosh, Ron. I can't even tell you how wonderful it's been," Cindy told him, glancing back at her students. "I could teach this every day of my life."

"Glad to hear that. I hoped it would be easy enough for you, especially since I made that print-out."

Cindy blushed, glancing toward the ground. "I'm sorry, Ron, but I didn't use that print-out. I'm an islander. I know the history of the Lilac Festival through and through. Plus, I wanted to add my own personality to the stories. I talked about my mother, planting lilacs in our back yard, and the year all the lilac bushes bloomed too early and ruined the festival for everyone except for the islanders."

"I didn't know about that," Ron said with a laugh. "I pity the festival organizer from that year. What a nightmare!"

"I bet it was," Cindy said contemplatively. "Like I said. We were kids. We just ran through the warm spring evenings and inhaled all the wonderful smells of lilac bushes and were grateful to do it all without the tourists around."

Behind her, Cindy's students had begun to finish up their planting and clean their hands of soil and gunk. Distracted, Cindy reached for a strand of hair to draw it around her ear, forgetting that her hands, too, were heavy with dirt.

"Oh, shoot," Cindy said, shaking her head to get the bits of dirt from her curls.

Ron's laughter rollicked across the cobblestones. "Now you're extra believable as the lilac-planting teacher."

"Or a run-away from the mental institution," Cindy joked. Just before she stepped back to finish out her class and give her closing statements, she added, "I am sorry I didn't use that print-out."

What she meant was: I know you put a lot of work into it. But trust me. I know better.

Ron shrugged. "It sounds like it would have interrupted your groove, anyway."

Cindy danced back to her group and announced that they'd finished for the morning. "But we have a jam-packed schedule of events the rest of the day. Ron Waters and the rest of the Lilac Festival committee have created such a stunning festival this year. I hope you find time to experience the island during its most exciting week of the year."

All the while, Ron watched her, his hands shoved deep in his pockets. A half-smile played out across his face. Cindy had to force herself to look away from him as his handsome face, and broad shoulders distracted her.

By Tuesday of the following week, Cindy had mastered the art of the lilac-planting seminar to such a degree that her class had become very popular, bursting at the seams with other lilac revelers who'd heard tell of her seminar and convinced themselves to wake up bright and early to join. Cindy had her speech down pat, easing from the history of lilacs to the Hubbard family, all the way to her personal stories of her mother, her daughter, and the rest of the islanders' experience of lilacs.

Midway through her tale of her daughter running headlong toward a large lilac bush so fast that she'd gotten herself all wrapped up in the flowers, sneezing herself to bits, a familiar couple walked past her group.

It was Michael and Margot.

Cindy stuttered with surprise, skipping a pivotal part of the story as she caught sight of them. Michael had his fingers laced through Margot's protectively, comfortably, as they turned to face Cindy, watching. Margot wore another beautiful summer dress, which stretched over her pregnant belly and fluttered toward the ground.

They were the perfect portrait of a Mackinac Island couple in the springtime, expectantly waiting for their family to gain its new member. Cindy had to force herself not to immediately reach for her camera to snap their photograph.

"Now, for this portion of the planting seminar, I need a volunteer," Cindy began, still stuttering slightly. Michael and Margot made her tongue twist with nerves.

Without pause, Margot brought her arm through the air to volunteer. "I'll do it," she said.

Cindy beckoned for Margot to approach, her heart thudding. Behind the group, Michael remained with his feet shoulder-width apart, and his arms crossed over his chest.

"I should be able to get myself down to the soil," Margot said, both to the crowd and Cindy herself. "But you might have to help me get up again."

Cindy laughed a little too long until tears formed in the corners of her eyes. Cupping Margot's elbow, she helped the young woman to her knees in front of the soil, where she rolled up the sleeves of her dress and blinked up at Cindy expectantly.

"The thing you have to remember about growing lilacs..." Cindy began, hardly remembering her prepared speech, "is that lilacs need between six and eight hours of sunlight per day. They also like alkaline soil and should be planted during either springtime after the ground thaws or autumn, right before the ground freezes."

As Cindy spoke, she and Margot illustrated how to prepare the soil to make it slowly more alkaline, then dug a hole twice as wide and just as deep as the root of the lilac. Bit by bit, Margot's fingernails filled with black soil, which contrasted dramatically against her porcelain skin. Occasionally, Cindy lifted her eyes to peer across the crowd and find Michael, still in the same spot, watching her. It reminded her of long-lost afternoons when Michael had played in the backyard as she'd planted her garden, running through the sprinkler system in only his underwear. "The kid has no responsibilities," Fred had said at the time. "He needs to learn to grow up."

After the lilac-planting seminar, Michael bustled up to help Margot to her feet. As she rose, she accidentally knocked several bulbs of black soil across Michael's white t-shirt. Margot's laugh rang out, gorgeous and song-like, as Michael tried to shake his t-shirt clean. It was no use.

Cindy had to force herself not to say something like, *Oh, I can take that for you, Michael. I'll have the stain out in no time.* Michael didn't want his mother's help with anything; that included laundry, too.

As the other students slowly headed away from the little sunny area where Cindy had set up the planting seminar, Michael and Margot stayed back, eyeing one another sheepishly. Cindy didn't want to put any pressure on them to leave and soon hopped back to gather her supplies, dropping bags of soil into the wheelbarrow and smacking her palms together to try to get the rest of the big chunks of dirt off.

"You know, Mom, you're not a bad teacher." Michael's voice rang out, nourishing and alive.

Cindy stopped short, her eyes on the wheelbarrow. Had he said that? Or had she dreamed it?

"Not that I should be so surprised," Michael continued. "You taught me so much over the years. How to ride a bike. How to bake a cake. How to—" He laughed at himself, gesturing again toward his stained t-shirt. "Well, I'm still not great at laundry."

"I'm there for stuff like that," Margot said proudly, her hand across her stomach. In a whisper, she added, "But it's only because I look for laundry tips online. Without the internet, I'd be lost."

Cindy laughed a little too loudly, shivering with fear. Why were they being so kind to her? What was this about?

"Mom..." Michael began suddenly, his tone shifting. "Margot showed me the photograph that you took of her that afternoon, reading."

Cindy's eyes filled with tears. "I'm sorry, again. It was rude of me to take a photograph of her. I just didn't even know it was her."

"No. That isn't what this is about," Michael countered. "Just... I had no idea how talented you were, Mom. All those years, you hardly took any photographs for yourself or your art. It made me wonder why you gave it all up."

Cindy remembered what Megan had told her down in East Lansing: *Michael deserves to know the truth about Jeremy.*

But that wasn't all.

Michael deserved to know that Fred wasn't his real father.

He deserved to know everything.

"I don't really know," Cindy whispered, caught in the storm of her mind. "I guess I just lost track of myself over the years. I'm fighting to get her back."

Michael nodded, furrowing his brow. He then glanced toward Margot, whose smile had faltered. Two twenty-somethings with a baby on the way couldn't possibly understand the devastation of a forty-seven-year-old woman, could they? It was silly that Cindy had even tried to tell them the truth.

"Well..." Michael began, clearly trying to end the conversation. His eyes grew cloudy as he placed his hand gently along Margot's back.

Cindy felt as though she watched her life crumbling before her eyes.

Say something. Anything to make him stay here with you a little while longer.

"Michael..." Cindy blurted his name, forcing Michael's eyes back toward hers.

Michael and Margot remained silent, captivated.

"I left your dad," Cindy heard herself say, her nostrils flared.

Michael furrowed his brow as Margot studied the ground between their feet. Along the cobblestone streets, tourists flocked excitedly, their voices ringing out with bright joy.

"I wouldn't blame you if you say it's too late for the two of us to mend our relationship," Cindy added, lifting her chin. "All I can do is try to convince you that I mean it this time. I want to be better. I want to be the mother I always should have been to you. Especially now."

I want to be a grandmother to your child.

She left this last sentiment unspoken. Michael closed his eyes against her words, clearly overwhelmed. In the distance, the ferry boat blared its horn, preparing to head back to the mainland.

"I don't know what to say," Michael whispered finally.

"I understand," Cindy offered, her throat tight.

"I just need time to process," Michael returned, his eyes sympathetic.

"Take all the time you need," Cindy murmured.

Michael nodded and bit down on his lower lip. Slowly, he and Margot turned back down the road, headed toward their little apartment. Margot stepped gingerly over the cobblestones as Michael walked slowly beside her, revealing a patience Cindy had never seen. He would be a remarkable father, the sort he should have had all along.

Chapter Seventeen

Cindy's Lilac Festival responsibilities came to a close around five-thirty that evening. Alone with nothing to do, no one to meet, and lost in thought, she wrapped her arms tightly across her chest and wandered through downtown, people-watching. She was most captivated by the families: little girls with ice cream cones, their fathers holding their free hands, mothers with sleeping babies swaddled across their chests, and exuberant children trying to rush ahead of their parents, only to race back when they grew frightened of the crowd.

Years and years ago, Cindy and Fred had taken Michael and Megan on a family vacation to Washington D.C., where they'd wandered through cherry blossom trees and gazed at the enormous monuments meant to honor the great men and women who'd made the United States what it was today. Megan had been seven, Michael ten. Michael had taken diligent notes about each monument, wanting to pause for a little too long at each to sketch a little view of the site. Fred had resisted this, gesturing with his camera as he said, "We have these for a reason. You don't have to draw it to remember it."

None of the fathers who walked with their sons and daughters through downtown Mackinac Island looked half as cruel as Fred had been back then. But what did Cindy know? So much happened behind closed doors. You could never really know a person until they let you in— and sometimes, when they let you in, that meant it was too late for you.

Could you ever really trust anyone?

At the far end of Main Street, there was an old flower shop, which had gone through the tides of many seasons for going on thirty years. Its front windows were perpetually filled with seasonal flowers and balloons that advertised recent holidays. HAPPY FATHER'S DAY currently sat front and center, ready for the June 19th weekend. *Father's Day*, Cindy thought. How ironic. She'd only ever forced Michael to celebrate the day for Fred, watching from behind as he'd carried Fred's present into the television room, disgruntled.

Had there ever been a time that Michael had loved his father? Or had Fred always created an environment of abuse and harsh words? How could any young boy come to love his father when faced with the facts of that world?

Cindy watched herself step through the door of the flower shop, which made the bell jangle overhead. An old woman with half-moon spectacles stepped out from the back, chewing at the edge of a cookie. She looked to need only a cookie a day to keep herself going; her bones poked from her skin, glowing translucent.

Cindy had met the woman several times but hadn't seen her around the island as of late, perhaps because she kept to herself in her little corner flower shop, tending to her cuttings and arranging beautiful bouquets. *Who needs the world when you have all of this?*

"Hello, Bethany," Cindy greeted.

"Hi, Cindy." The woman had aged a good ten years since Cindy had last seen her. "What can I help you with today? Is someone in your family celebrating a birthday?"

"Not exactly." Cindy's heart thudded with sorrow. "I need three bouquets, please. Your finest flowers, with plenty of lilacs filtered in."

Bethany slid her half-moon glasses down her nose. "No particular instructions?"

Cindy shook her head, her eyes to the window that looked out across the Straits of Mackinac. Her heart ballooned in her chest. In the silence, Bethany seemed to understand what she meant.

These flowers weren't meant for the living.

Cindy waited for a good forty-five minutes as Bethany prepared the arrangements. By the time she'd paid and returned to the dewy streets with her three bouquets, she'd dropped two hundred and twelve dollars and killed nearly too much time. But the Mackinac Island cemetery didn't close till sundown— which gave Cindy plenty of time.

Armed with three bouquets, Cindy walked like a ghost through the families of downtown Mackinac and headed east toward the cemetery. She hadn't tended to her beloved family and friends in over two months, at least, and felt heavy with regret— cursing herself for getting too hung up on her own worthless drama to go to Sainte Anne's Cemetery.

If anything in the world mattered, it was her memories. She wouldn't forget that again.

Cindy charted her path through the cemetery, headed first toward her mother's more recent grave. The grave was located in the "Swartz Family" area, where there was enough space set aside for Alex, Tracey, Cindy, and Dean. It was strange to stand above the ground in which you'd be buried one day. Cindy had heard others say it was a comfort to them, knowing where they'd be. Megan would come to this very place to put flowers on Cindy's own grave, maybe even with children of her own.

Cindy dropped to her knees at her mother's grave to trace the lettering. MANDY SWARTZ. Her teeth digging into her lower lip, Cindy contemplated the sorrow of her mother's life. Dean and Mandy had loved one another, but had it been a real and nourishing love? Compared to the love between Jeremy and Cindy, she wasn't so sure.

"Hi, Mom. I'm sorry that I've stayed away so long." Cindy's nostrils flared as she lifted her eyes toward the remaining light in the sky above her. "You probably know everything that's happened— that I left Fred, finally. And that I'm thinking about telling Michael the truth." Cindy's heart thumped away, such a contrast to the graves around her. "You're probably thinking, you silly girl! Why didn't you tell him before? I have no idea what to say to that. I wanted to build a family like the Swartz family. But if there's anything I've learned over the past nine months since Elise got here, it's that our family was certainly not perfect, either. I should have just leaned into the truth."

Cindy stretched her palm out across her mother's grave. She wished it felt like something besides chilly stone.

"It isn't fair what Dad did to you," Cindy whispered. "But I know he loved you. And after the whole thing with Allison blew over, he honored you in everything he did. I don't know how much that counts for anything, especially after all you gave to us, especially Alex."

Cindy remained in front of her mother's grave for another few minutes, trying to feel what it had felt like to be next to her before she'd passed on. Mandy, her beautiful mother. Mandy was the most generous woman she'd ever met. Did she have any of her characteristics? Did people see Cindy and think, *Mandy would be so proud?*

Now down to only two bouquets, Cindy headed for the

grave on the far side of the cemetery. Recently, someone had placed a single red rose in front of it— proof that Wayne was always heavy with loss, even though he'd decided to fall in love again. The rose warmed Cindy's jagged heart.

"Hi, Tara." Cindy sat cross-legged in front of the grave, her shoulders dropping forward. She felt the way she had when they'd been teenagers, seated cross-legged on the floor of their mothers' kitchens with uncooked cookie dough between them. "You'd make fun of me for missing you as much as I do. You'd say, 'Pull it together, Swartz,' and then pour me a glass of wine and make me dance to Madonna. You were always a little too good at getting me to forget myself and the world."

Cindy sniffled and splayed the flowers a few inches to the left of the flower Wayne had left behind.

"I don't know how much Wayne tells you about his current life," Cindy whispered. "For a long time, I resented him for having any kind of happiness that didn't include you. I know you wouldn't be happy with me for feeling that way. When you met Wayne, I remember you told me something about 'loving in a way that makes other people feel free.' I couldn't understand what you meant, especially because I was locked in the confines of my marriage to Fred. But now that I've stepped out of it, I realize the way I allowed 'love' to lock me away for decades. Because your love for Wayne was so nourishing, so true, he's been allowed to continue to live— probably feeling your blessing in everything he does. If that isn't proof that you're a better woman than me, I don't know what is."

Cindy's voice cracked. She closed her eyes, pressing the tips of her fingers against her temples. She could have lingered in front of that grave for another two hours, digging into a monologue about the disappointments and sorrows she'd experienced. *If only I could hear your voice one more time. If only you could make fun of me one more time, or hold my hand on the back porch, or surprise me with your nourishing and thoughtful words.*

Sunlight dipped lower in the evening sky, casting everything in a ghoulish light. The weight of passing time felt especially heavy in the graveyard. Faced with the coming closure of the cemetery, Cindy rose, brushed off her knees of soil, and headed toward the back corner of the cemetery— an area she'd strictly avoided in the years since Tara and Mandy's deaths.

Compared to Mandy and Tara's, Jeremy Miller's gravestone was a slight stone, barely peeking up out of the ground. Twenty-five years ago, Jeremy's family hadn't had more than a few pennies to rub together but had scrounged up all they could to place him forever beneath the old oak, where he could find "forever shade." Dean Swartz had offered money to the Millers, but they'd refused it out of pride. A year after Jeremy's death, his mother had passed on as well, leaving Jeremy's father heartsick and emotionally cold. He'd eventually joined his brother in Detroit, never returning to the island again.

"1997." Cindy read the year of his death aloud, mesmerized by how "recent" the year sounded to her own ears. *How had twenty-five years already passed?* She could fully remember entering the decade of the nineties, blissfully unaware of the cruelty of adulthood fast approaching.

"Jeremy." Cindy's eyes immediately watered up as though she'd been slapped. She folded herself in front of his grave, holding onto her knees as she gazed forward, trying to visualize his face.

Finally, she forced herself to say what she'd come to the cemetery to say.

"I don't know why I never told him," Cindy whispered. "I was so devastated to lose you, and I guess I thought, if I could make up a story around my life, one that sounded nicer than reality, I could start to believe in it and forget. But the truth is, you never really forget anything, do you? Even though I tried to bury you so deeply in the past, you were always an element of the present— one of the direct reasons why Michael and Fred never saw eye-to-eye. As Michael got older, I watched your emotions play out across his face. I heard your sense of humor come out of him, something Fred resented more than anything, I think. There's nothing worse than watching your adopted son become funnier than you ever could be."

Cindy's heart twisted. Above her, a sparrow flashed to an outstretched limb of the oak. It twittered down at her as though it warned her about the closure of the cemetery. There was never enough time.

"I still remember what you told me when I first broke the news that I was pregnant," Cindy whispered. "I was terrified of what would happen, especially because it seemed like we never had enough money for the two of us, let alone a brand-new baby. You held me as I fell asleep that night and then held me even tighter when I woke up, breathless and scared, just past midnight. 'You can't worry yourself about bad things that haven't happened yet,' you said, which seems so haunting now, after your accident. But I think since then, I've lived in constant fear that something bad is lurking around the corner. It's made me handicapped in my own life. And Jeremy... I don't want to be handicapped anymore. I've loved you in a devastating and secret way for decades. Maybe now, I want to love you and our story in a different way. Maybe now, I want to set myself free."

Minutes later, through Cindy's silence came the sound of a fence clacking against itself. Cindy jumped to her feet and glanced back to find the cemetery gardener closing for the night. Already, night stars sparkled through a darkening sky. Where had the time gone?

Cindy stretched out her forty-seven-year-old legs and rushed for the entrance, waving a hand through the dark. Just in the nick of time, the gardener spotted her and flung the fence open again.

"I didn't see you back there in the corner," the gardener said simply, as though nobody had gone back to the area of Jeremy's grave in many years.

Outside the now-locked cemetery, Cindy latched her hands across her knees and gasped for breath. She hadn't sprinted like that in quite some time. She then lifted her shoulders back, drawing her eyes toward the heavy moon on high. A thought struck her, suddenly yet very clearly, that it wasn't time to give up on her life quite yet. There was so much, still, to live for.

Chapter Eighteen

At the base of Fort Mackinac, a twenty-something guitarist sat strumming an old Green Day song. "Tattoos of memories and dead skin on trial; for what it's worth, it was worth all the while." His voice was craggy and thick with emotion, and he drew an immense crowd of revelers, who swayed in time to the song. Their faces shone with the light of the overhead streetlamps. Together, they looked like part of a dream.

Cindy paused at the outer ring of listeners, allowing the strumming to take hold of her heart. Jeremy had been an occasional guitarist, sometimes chasing her around the house as he played and sang. How her heart ached for those memories.

As the last bars of the song strummed out, Cindy glanced leftward to find a familiar face in the crowd. Ron Waters stood with his hands shoved deep in his pockets, his eyes glistening as he listened to the guitarist. Cindy half-considered ducking away from Ron, especially after the emotional tide of her trip to the cemetery and the conversation with Michael. But hadn't she only just told Jeremy that she wanted to live again?

As the guitarist began another nineties tune, Cindy hustled around the half-circle of listeners and patted Ron on the shoulder. Ron leaped back, shock playing out across his face. "Oh! Cindy!"

"Shhh!" an older woman nearby hissed at him, annoyed that he'd interrupted the song.

Ron snickered with laughter and hustled back toward the water, drawing Cindy along with him. Cindy cackled along with him, feeling like a schoolgirl who'd just gotten in trouble for talking in class.

"What are you doing out here?" Ron finally asked her, swiping a tear from beneath his eye.

"Just on a walk," Cindy lied. Her heart lifted toward her throat.

"Same. I need daily mental health walks during the Lilac Festival, otherwise, I lose my cool."

Cindy's grin widened. "Mental health walks are essential. But have you heard about mental health drinks at The Pink Pony? They can't be beat."

Ron's eyes glittered with intrigue. Cindy's stomach clenched and unclenched as she listened back to the words she'd just said. *Did I just ask him out?*

"I've heard of these mental health drinks." Ron countered. "I think I'd like to give them a try."

When Cindy and Ron appeared in the doorway of The Pink Pony, Marcy dragged her bifocal glasses to the bridge of her nose and assessed them. Cindy laughed inwardly, remembering the very same Marcy who'd watched her on her dates with Jeremy, then her dates with Fred. As the bartender of The Pink Pony, Marcy had a front-seat view of the ever-changing lives of Mackinac Island residents. She could have written eight hundred books.

As Marcy poured a glass of wine for Cindy and a pint of beer for Ron, Cindy sat nervously across from Ron, crossing and uncrossing her legs and praying to think of something clever to say. Ron seemed just about as nervous, checking his watch and then his phone and then his watch again.

Was this nervous energy all because of their flirtatious sunset boat trip?

Or was Cindy only imagining the strangeness between them?

"The planting seminars have gone really well," Cindy finally announced.

"I've gotten about a thousand compliments. Makes me a little embarrassed, honestly. It almost feels like you should oversee the Lilac Festival rather than me. You're the queen of the lilacs," Ron said.

Cindy's cheeks burned with embarrassment. Marcy arrived a second later and tapped both drinks on their table, giving them a mischievous smile. Cindy lifted her drink toward Ron's, clinked it, and said, "Here's to you, taking a chance on me."

Ron furrowed his brow, incredulous. "What do you mean? Taking a chance on you? You were never a chance. You were always so clearly perfect for the job."

For a long moment, Cindy's lips parted with surprise. A roar swelled up from the back area of her mind. *Pull it together, Cindy. Come on. It's not a big deal.*

Ron's words might have been simple or easy for someone else to hear.

But for Cindy, who was fresh off twenty-five years of failed romance and resentments and hiding away, the sentiment was too powerful.

Cindy's face scrunched up as tears rolled down her cheeks. She splayed her hands across the table as her shoulders shook. Ron, realizing he'd said something off, placed his beer back on the table and hurriedly said, "Are you okay? Cindy, gosh, I'm sorry if I said something wrong."

Cindy shook her head as a million images flashed through

her mind: Fred, turning away from her in bed; Michael, saying goodbye and leaving the island for three years; Margot, pregnant on the bench down the road, carrying Cindy and Jeremy's grandchild; Jeremy, when he'd first taken her hand on that particularly chilly day during their pre-teen years...

"I'm so sorry," Cindy coughed. "I don't know what's come over me."

Ron grabbed a handkerchief from his back pocket and placed it delicately in her hand. "It's clean, don't worry."

Cindy mopped herself up and blew her nose loudly, a noise that made her laugh and cry at once. "Gosh, I'm such a mess."

Ron shook his head. "I've seen worse."

"I don't know about that. But thank you." Cindy blew her nose again, shoving away all thoughts of embarrassment. She had a hunch that Marcy had turned up the volume on the speaker system to distract the other guests from Cindy's outbursts. Bless her.

"To be honest with you, I just came from the cemetery," Cindy whispered.

Ron took the news without hesitation, as though he'd been prepared to carry her story all this time. His eyes showed the tenderness of his heart, proof that he had enough empathy for anything she might say.

"I've spent a fair amount of time in cemeteries, myself," Ron said. "I think the strangest part of visiting my wife's grave is how not weird it is, sometimes, to sit there in front of the stone and tell her everything that's on my mind."

His wife. He'd lost his wife.

How much strength it must have taken to remove the wedding ring...

Cindy tilted her head knowingly, thinking back to what she'd said to Tara, her mother, and finally, Jeremy. You had to have experienced true loss to understand what it meant to sit before a gravestone and deliver the contents of your heart to the air around you, praying they heard you. They had to hear you, wherever they were. Right?

"I'm so sorry to hear about your wife," Cindy finally managed, her voice cracking.

Ron nodded, clenching his fist across the table. "I never know what to say to that."

"I understand," Cindy breathed. "When my boyfriend died, I had no idea how to manage my own emotions, let alone other people's. I remember my mother sobbing at his funeral as I rubbed her back, wondering why it wasn't the other way around. I just felt so numb, especially when people tried to tell me how sorry they were..." Cindy sniffed into his handkerchief and then corrected herself. "Not that I didn't appreciate that they cared."

"Your boyfriend..." Ron whispered. "How old were you?"

"Twenty-two," Cindy offered. "He'd been my first everything. We started dating when we were thirteen and just kept going. We were basically living together at the time of the accident."

Cindy's story spilled from between her lips. Slowly, her heart began to dispel its darkness. She thought back to what Tracey had said about just finally talking about her past trauma. She'd clearly had a point.

"That must have been so traumatic," Ron offered gently. "The kind of thing that changes you forever."

"It did," Cindy whispered, dropping her eyes to the table. "And even now, as I get up the confidence to divorce my husband, I still mourn Jeremy. It's strange. I thought marriage and children would completely blot out the past sorrows. Turns out, you carry those sorrows with you, wherever you go and whatever you do."

Ron closed his eyes so that his long lashes flashed across his cheeks. Cindy wanted to reach out and spread her hand across his still-clenched fist but held herself back.

"You'll love Jeremy forever," Ron said simply. "Just like I'll love Rose forever."

Cindy nodded. "I wish I could reach into my heart and find the space I had for Fred, my husband. If it was still there somewhere, I'd at least be able to rationalize the decisions I made."

"Your children," Ron pointed out. "They're enough, aren't they?"

Cindy's throat tightened. "My daughter, yes. She's a dream. Headed off to pursue her dreams at Michigan State University this autumn. It breaks my heart that she's headed away, but I know it's all a part of her process of finding herself. That's something I never really managed to do."

"You should be proud," Ron murmured. His eyes flickered as he then asked, "And your son?"

"My son is much more difficult," Cindy whispered, her voice hardly loud enough for even herself to hear. She turned her eyes toward Marcy to find that she leaned heavily off the bar, eavesdropping.

It's not like she doesn't know my secrets already.

"Michael isn't Fred's son," Cindy said, surprising herself with her own clarity. She lifted her eyes to meet Ron's, waiting for shock to play out across his face.

But Ron offered her no sense of shock or alarm.

He only said, "He's Jeremy's gift to you."

The words wrapped tightly around Cindy's heart, squeezing it so tight she thought it might burst. As her eyes filled with tears, she whispered, "That's it. He's a gift. He's been a gift all along. But the thing is, I've never told him the truth."

"The truth can be a difficult thing to face," Ron whispered, unclenching his fist to reach it across the table and wrap it tenderly over hers. "But if Michael has half as much goodness in him as you do, he'll find a way to understand. It might take some time — but you owe him that."

Cindy's hand flooded from the warmth of his palm. It was only with his hand on hers that she realized just how chilly she'd been.

"It took me months to figure out that my wife was really and truly gone," Ron breathed. "I realized that I listened for her to come home at her usual time. I woke up in the middle of the night and reached for her in bed. I even picked up my phone to call her as recently as a few weeks ago." Ron laughed inwardly. "The Lilac Festival is my way to hold onto her memory. It's my way to honor her. Thank you for having a part in that."

Overwhelmed by his story, Cindy leaped from her chair and fell into Ron's arms. His palm stretched across the curls of her hair; another wrapped tightly at the small of her back. Together, they held one another somberly as the bar's many drinkers rolled around them, cackling. It was like they'd stepped from this world and into the next.

When their hug broke, Cindy used Ron's handkerchief to tap at the outer edges of her eyes, conscious that she was probably covered in eye makeup. Ron seemed not to notice.

"You should stand on the Lilac Festival Parade Float with me this Saturday," he said finally, surprising her so much that she laughed gently.

"I know it sounds silly," Ron continued. "But we've both put so much of ourselves into this year's festival. It wouldn't make sense without you by my side."

Cindy tilted her head as her smile fell. For a long moment, she and Ron locked eyes. *A future together, Ron and I? Is that so outside the bounds of possibilities? Is that an insane thing to dream of?*

"I'd love to, Ron," Cindy finally told him. "I'll see you at the parade."

Chapter Nineteen

Three hours before Cindy was set to arrive downtown for the annual Lilac Festival Parade, Emma and Megan barrelled through the doorway of Tracey's little house, armed with strawberries, bananas, and yogurt. As the sunlight of the June morning glittered into the kitchen, Emma and Megan chatted joyously, whirring together smoothies for the four of them — nutrients and vitamins to kick-start this very important day.

"You'll need a blender when you move to East Lansing," Cindy said, putting on her "mom" voice as she watched Megan shake the light pink smoothie into four glasses. "Wait, I'll put it on the list." Cindy ruffled through her purse on the hunt for the notepad she'd begun to use for Megan's GOING TO EAST LANSING list.

"You know, Mom, you can use the notes app on your phone." Megan teased her mother as she placed the smoothie glass next to Cindy, who clicked at a blue pen before scribing: BLENDER.

"If I write it on my phone, there's no way I'll be able to find it again," Cindy joked.

"But it's not like you'll find the notepad in your purse, either," Tracey countered, entering in her light pink robe and patting Megan on the shoulder. "You should have seen her the other day, searching for her keys in the bottom of that thing. Took you, what, ten minutes?"

Cindy laughed, dropping her head back. "We did have to dump the contents of my purse onto the porch." she confessed.

"You're so organized in all other areas of your life," Emma teased. "Why is the purse your only black hole?"

"I contain multitudes," Cindy quipped as she finished scribing BLENDER on the bottom of a list that included things like bed sheets, pillows, towels, pots and pans, and "a new raincoat," which was underlined four times. Cindy wouldn't have her girl dripping wet as she scampered across campus.

As they sipped their smoothies, the four Swartz women sat out on the porch in the shade, watching the breeze shift through the branches of the maple tree in the front yard. A large lilac bush hung heavy with purple along the street, a gorgeous reminder to enjoy the season they were in.

"Do you mind if we leave the Lilac Festival a bit early to head out to the party later?" Megan asked Tracey and Cindy, eyeing them mischievously.

"You mean the exclusive twenty-something party across the island?" Cindy said with a laugh. "I haven't been to that party since... 1998? Something like that?"

"Same," Tracey said, shivering with laughter. "I wonder what it's like these days."

Megan and Emma locked eyes to have an intimate "cousin" conversation across the table. Cindy could half-guess that they were bubbling with excitement for the approaching party, with its bonfire and its beautiful, suntanned guests, many of whom would be handsome men.

"Remember that one year that Jeremy did a keg stand at the party?" Tracey asked Cindy.

Emma and Megan, who were now both privy to the "Jeremy topic," yanked their heads around, burning with curiosity about this Jeremy fellow.

"He did," Cindy assured them. "Everyone always said the party started when he arrived and ended when he left. As his girlfriend, this was exhausting."

"Oh, come on. You loved every single minute," Tracey told her.

Cindy's heart swelled with memory. She stared into the smoothie for a split-second too long as a quiet settled over the table.

"Marcy had a few things to say about you last night," Tracey said suddenly. "Maybe hinting that the good old days are here again."

Cindy's cheeks burned at the memory of her and Ron's "overly long" embrace a few nights before. She glanced toward Megan as regret swirled in her stomach. But Megan just shook her head. Her eyes were rimmed red.

"You deserve whatever goodness is coming to you, Mom," Megan breathed. "Please, don't worry about me."

Cindy dressed in a light purple dress that, admittedly, showed a tiny bit more of her muscular legs than most dresses she owned. When she stepped back out onto the porch after her change, Emma, Megan, and Tracey howled with delight, demanding that she spin around in circles to show off.

"Good thing you'll be on a float today at the parade," Tracey teased. "Everyone needs to see you looking like this. Everyone."

"Cindy Swartz is back!" Megan howled.

Cindy grabbed a spring jacket, waved goodbye to her biggest fans, and scampered down the street to where the Lilac Festival Parade began, right outside the Grand Hotel, located just east of the Pontiac Trail Head, where the homes she'd grown up and raised her children in were located. Her heart burned with adrenaline as she glanced westward, back to that gorgeous house Fred had purchased for them all those years ago. *Am I really giving all that up?*

But just as her hesitations began to balloon in her stomach, Ron stepped out from behind a carriage. He was dressed in a tuxedo with a light purple tie, and his thick salt and pepper hair (around the bald spot) was styled handsomely with a gel that brought out the slight curls. Cindy's heart smashed against her ribcage, threatening to jump out. He really was something.

"Hi, there." Ron greeted her with a nervous smile, which only made him more handsome. His eyes scanned her dress and then jumped back up as though he was embarrassed that he'd allowed himself to notice. "You look beautiful."

"Thank you." Cindy's cheeks burned at the concept of a compliment. *When was the last time Fred had given her one?*

Ron stepped back to gesture out across the floats, most of which were attached to carriages. Horses bucked their heads back to make their shining hair waft through the wind.

"This is our float," Ron said, pointing to the very last and more ornate float, which featured beautiful paper-maché lilac bushes designed by local artists. There were two "thrones" on the float itself, and both were lined with fake gold.

"It's like we're prom king and queen," Cindy joked as she stepped up to try out the throne on the right-hand side.

"It's silly, I know," Ron said, settling in beside her. "But the parade needs a lot of pomp and circumstance. Look at how big the marching band is this year!"

Sixty-some members of a nearby Upper Peninsula marching band had assembled for the parade, dressed in white and blue with shimmering yellow tassels. The teenagers were playful and laughing, still not in line for the parade. In front of them, a number of baton throwers and cheerleaders had gathered, gossiping in a circle. Other floats included the Mackinac Island Artist Council, the Mackinac Island Bird Watcher's Association, and the Mackinac Island Community Outreach Program. The parade would wrap twice around downtown before culminating near the docks, where a party would begin.

"Not long now!" The woman in charge of the parade hollered for the marching band to line up and the baton-throwers to set up around them. She tapped the head cheer-leader on the shoulder, which forced her to send instructions back to her troupe.

"I feel kind of silly," Cindy said as the front carriage began to jump forward, drawing the rest of the line toward downtown.

Ron wrapped his fingers through hers coaxingly, giving her an earnest smile. "Then you're doing it exactly right."

"You just wanted someone to go through this embarrass-ment with you, didn't you?" Cindy teased.

Ron laughed. "You can see right through me, can't you?"

"No way! I wish," Cindy countered. "Although maybe that would make everything a little too easy."

There they were again: dancing around the subject of their brewing flirtation. *It's too soon for both of us*, Cindy thought. *He's still torn up from his wife's death, and I'm only in the first steps of separating from my husband. But gosh, it's nice to have his hand on mine. Gosh, it's nice to hear his laugh, to feel not-so-alone in this strange world.*

"Where'd your head go?" Ron teased her as the horses clopped forward.

Cindy's smile widened from ear to ear. "Just thinking about how nice it is to sit here next to you."

Did I really say that?

The marching band began to play an old John Philip Sousa tune, something Cindy had heard over a thousand times yet never learned the name of. The baton twirlers began to twirl their glittery batons, tossing them into the air and catching nearly all of them (with only a few dropping them to the ground). At this, Cindy chuckled and whispered to Ron, "If I had thrown that thing in the air, I would have dropped it immediately. No doubt in my mind."

"Same," Ron agreed with a smirk.

A crowd had gathered on either side of the parade route, thick with Mackinac Island tourists who waved American flags and wore little lilac-themed pins. They waved their hands at Ron and Cindy, who stood to wave back, sometimes using one another to steady themselves.

Probably the tourists think we're together. I wonder if they think we look good together. I wonder if they think this is right.

Occasionally, the carriage hit a rickety bit of cobblestone road, casting both Cindy and Ron back to their chairs. They shivered with laughter as they continued to wave their hands, bug-eyed, to greet the tourists. The marching band continued to play, although it seemed like they only knew one song and repeated it over and over again.

"I guess I should ask more about the marching band's plans next year," Ron said with a laugh.

"Next year..." Cindy arched her eyebrow as a few cobblestones bounced them again. "Do you think..."

"That we can do it better than ever?" Ron asked. "Yes. I've thought about it extensively. We should start meetings about the schedule early. Maybe January?"

"November, to keep it safe," Cindy told him.

"I guess that means I'll have to stick around the island over winter."

"I guess so," Cindy said with a playful shrug.

"Won't that be terrible?" Ron's voice was heavy with sarcasm.

"I don't know. I've never spent a winter off the island," Cindy said. "I guess you'll have to tell me what it's like for you.

I have a top-secret hot chocolate recipe just in case you need a bit of help to get you through."

"That should do the trick."

After looping down Main Street and Market Street twice and waving at upwards of seven hundred tourists, the parade finished outright beneath Fort Mackinac, near the ferry docks. Ron leaped out of the float first before lifting a hand to help Cindy down gently. As she dropped toward the ground, her eyes connected with Tracey's, where she stood with Emma, Megan, Dean, Alex, and Elise at the base of Fort Mackinac. They smiled blissfully, happy for their Cindy— a woman on the up-and-up.

A little stage had been set up in front of the docks, upon which a quintet of string instruments played "Take Me to Mackinac Island" by John Manikoff. As the song petered out, Ron dropped down to whisper, "Wish me luck," right before he bounded on stage with the spirit of a much younger man.

Imagine living life with that man. Imagine the boundless possibilities of each and every day, especially after you'd both experienced such loss and made it through.

After the song finished, the crowd that had gathered around the stage roared, regretfully giving up their applause after nearly five minutes. Ron remained on stage, clapping along with the rest of the tourists and gesturing to the quintet joyfully.

Finally, as the noise depleted, Ron stepped up to the microphone and spoke.

"That's the thing about the Lilac Festival. It draws together some of the most talented people across the state of Michigan, all here to celebrate these gorgeous flowers. As I recently learned from a dear friend..."

Here, his eyes locked onto Cindy's, who stood alongside their parade float, nervously shifting her weight.

"I learned that some of the lilac bushes here on Mackinac

Island were planted in the 1800s and aren't showing any signs of giving up yet. It's a beautiful thing, the density of history that Mackinac Island gifts us. And it's up to us to appreciate it in any way we can."

Again, the crowd roared joyously, pounding their hands together. Cindy, too, cried out over the applause, surprising herself with her own happiness. When was the last time she'd felt it like this, like a wave overtaking her? For too long, she'd lived life deep in the shadows.

Ron's speech continued, during which he thanked each and every member of the Lilac Festival committee before finishing out with a call-out to Cindy. "I'd like to give a final thank you to Cindy Swartz, whose commitment to this island and this festival is unparalleled. I have a hunch that very soon, she'll take over the festival for herself. In the meantime, she allows me to pretend to handle things."

The crowd tittered and glanced toward where Ron gestured. Cindy waved a hand, catching sight of the bartender, Marcy, off to the left of the crowd, still in her bartending outfit. She gave Cindy a firm and knowing nod, yet again front row seat to Cindy's ever-changing world.

"What many of you islanders probably don't know is that Cindy is also a very talented photographer," Ron continued as Cindy's cheeks burned with embarrassment. "Unbeknownst to her, I've managed to gather more than fifty photographers she's taken, some demonstrating the history of nineties on Mackinac Island and some taken over the past several weeks. When placed side-by-side, you can feel the many ways the island has shifted over the years; but, more interestingly, you can also feel the many ways it hasn't changed at all— that it's flowed through season after season, from generation to generation, with immense love and tenderness and joy. They're on display at the Market Street Gallery, and they're must-sees for this summer season."

Here, Ron looked at Cindy once more, giving her a sneaky smile. Cindy's heart nearly shattered with surprise.

My photographs? On display? In an exhibition?

After Ron finished his speech, he stepped down from the podium and headed back toward Cindy. Her heart swelled in her throat. But before he could reach her, another Lilac Festival committee organizer stepped between them to congratulate Ron on his tremendous success. Cindy glanced toward her feet, feeling suddenly like an outsider on her own island.

"Mom?"

The voice rang out from the crowd somewhere to the left of her. At first, Cindy hardly registered it, as it was a word thrown around by countless people countless times per day. She wasn't necessarily the "mom" in need.

"Cindy! Mom!"

Finally, Cindy jumped around to find Michael and Margot, trying their best to weave through the bustling crowd. The marching band had begun to play "America" by Simon and Garfunkel, which mentioned Michigan.

"Michigan seems like a dream to me now..." the crowd sang along, saying the Michigan part extra-loud, with extra passion.

Michael looked tanned and muscular yet oddly nervous. He looked to try to protect Margot from the chaos of the crowd, guarding her and pressing people to the side. Margot's pregnant belly seemed even a little bigger than a few days ago and made the skirt of her dress flutter around her thighs.

For a long moment, Cindy wasn't sure why Michael had approached her. She stared at him as her eyes filled with tears. But when he reached her, he extended his arms out on either side so that she could fall forward into him, lost in the strength of his hug.

For years, I had to carry you in my arms. You were so helpless, the son of the only man I'd ever loved. I did my best. I thought what I'd done was right...

"Mom, this is incredible," Michael finally said, stepping back as he swiped a tear from his cheek. "The parade was beautiful. The baton twirlers were amazing."

"Everything was beautiful," Cindy agreed.

"It's amazing what you've done," Michael said.

"And an exhibition!" Margot cried. "I can't wait to go see your work."

"I should really have a word with your Aunt Tracey," Cindy said, half-joking. "I don't know how she got a hand on all my old photographs."

"Mom, it's a blessing. Someone had to put your work out there if you weren't willing to," Michael offered.

Cindy scrunched up her face, struggling not to cry. As she swallowed the lump in her throat, Margot stepped back gently and nodded toward Michael. It was a sign.

"Mom," Michael began tentatively. "I've thought about what you said after the planting seminar. And to be honest with you... there's a lot I want to talk to you about. A lot I still need to say. But I'd be willing to try."

I can finally tell him the truth. It'll be the hardest thing in the world. But it'll finally be his to know.

"Thank you, Michael," Cindy whispered, breathless. "I have so many things I need to tell you, too."

Mother and son smiled at one another. Cindy slid a curl behind her ear as the sunlight caught Margot's gorgeous hair. After a terrible ending of the Simon and Garfunkel song, the marching band burst into another classic Michigan favorite, "All Summer Long."

"It was summertime in Northern Michigan..." Michael sang along teasingly. "Gosh, this was huge when I was a teenager."

"It was huge in Texas, too. Never thought I'd make it up to Northern Michigan." Margot countered. "Guess you never really know where life will take you."

But as they swam in the idyllic beauty of that Saturday afternoon, there was a sudden and violent snap. Cindy turned to find a tanned and muscular man whipping through the crowd, smacking himself into people who didn't get out of his way quickly enough. His eyes were animalistic, and his motions were sloppy yet violent— proof that he was too drunk to care exactly who he hurt.

Oh my God. What will Fred do to us?

Is this his revenge?

He couldn't just sit in that house all by himself while the rest of us prospered.

He never allowed us to be happy before. Why would he allow it now?

"Hey! Hey! Security!" Ron howled into the speaker system as Fred bustled toward Cindy. "Get that man!"

Fred hadn't thought about security. He'd thought, as usual, that his violent tendencies could get him through. He continued to press forward as Cindy backed toward the float. Michael ducked in between Fred and Cindy, his fists bare.

"Get back, Dad!" Michael called angrily.

On cue, two security guards made their way to Fred and wrapped his arms behind his back. Cindy's heart pounded fearfully as Ron hustled up to align himself with Cindy and Michael. Fred hissed and spat like a cat on the verge of attacking. He then actually spat on the ground at Michael's feet.

"What the hell did you just call me?" Fred asked icily.

Cindy recognized this mood. This was the drunken version of Fred, who would start a fire just to watch the world burn for the pleasure of it.

The security guards began to tug Fred away from the rest of the crowd, where Officer Ben waited in the wings, prepared to reprimand Fred. In truth, Fred hadn't done anything quite yet besides storm through the crowd. They probably couldn't hold him for anything.

"Just stay away from us!" Michael called to him. "We don't want anything to do with you."

Fred glared at Michael, then turned his eyes pointedly toward Cindy. *In sickness and in health. Forever and ever, amen.* They'd taken vows. How had everything gone so terribly wrong?

"That's a fine way to talk to the man who agreed to adopt you," Fred blurted then, his nostrils flared.

Cindy's heart dropped to the base of her stomach. Here it was: the truth. And instead of telling Michael the proper way, easing him into it, Fred had gone out of his way to destroy the fledgling relationship between Michael and Cindy. He'd pointed at the sharpest pain of her life and laughed at it.

This was so typical Fred.

"That's right," Fred said, just before the security guards dragged him too far from sight. "You're two peas in a pod, you and your mother. I'll be better off without you, a brat nobody could ever love."

Chapter Twenty

The fall-out from that afternoon of the Lilac Festival Parade seemed insurmountable.

Just after Fred's confession that he wasn't Michael's actual father and that Cindy had kept this news from her son for his entire life, Michael looked shell-shocked. He gaped at Cindy for a long moment as Margot wrapped her arms around his waist, begging him to calm down.

"Tell me you haven't lied to me all this time?" Michael finally spat out, just as angry as Fred had been, but in a quiet way.

Cindy only nodded her head as her eyes welled with tears. "There's so much you don't know. Please, let me explain."

But Michael couldn't speak after that. Margot laced her fingers through his and coaxed him away while Cindy turned to find Tracey there beside her, her arms lifting to wrap Cindy in a warm hug. Over the top of them, the marching band music seemed overly loud, making it difficult for Cindy to hear much more than Tracey's, "Let's get out of here."

In the days after the parade, Cindy sat listlessly around

Tracey's house, incapable of doing much more than feeding herself, watching television, and texting Michael with a simple:

CINDY: Please. Let me explain.

"He'll come around," Tracey told Cindy, her voice lined with doubt. "He loves you. And shouldn't it be a good thing for him to learn that Fred isn't his father? He hates Fred. This gives him permission to hate him even more."

A true friend, Ron had offered his support as best as he could. Three times over a week and a half, he came to Tracey's with bottles of wine and little snacks and tried to chat about other topics, anything to get Cindy's head out of its swirling darkness. Cindy laughed several times, surprising herself by allowing herself, for a split second, to forget.

When Ron departed for the evening, Tracey stepped out onto the porch to join Cindy for a final glass of wine. It was now mid-June, and, very soon, filming would begin on the island for Elise's movie. Tracey was heavy in preparation mode for the next weeks as she tore into a brand-new field of "movie magic." "Everything has to be perfect," Tracey said nervously, studying a list of odds and ends that were essential for purchasing for the scenes in the two-hour-long film. "You could never imagine how many bow ties you'd need for a movie."

Cindy couldn't manage much more than to nod in return.

"Ron always looks so forlorn when he leaves," Tracy pointed out as she folded up her list. "Like leaving you is the worst thing that could have ever happened to him."

"He just doesn't have that many friends," Cindy countered. "Not that I do..."

"You know everyone on this island, Cindy Swartz. Don't pretend that you don't."

"Well." Cindy adjusted her sweatshirt and zipped it to her chin. "It's been a true pleasure getting to know Ron. He's not like anyone else I've ever met..."

Tracey tilted her head.

"What's that look for?" Cindy demanded.

"Nothing. It's just that... I hope you find a way to allow yourself to be happy again. Whatever that means for you," Tracey tried.

Cindy's throat tightened. Before she could properly respond, her cell phone buzzed on the end of the table. As she reached for it, her heart hammered with hope. *Could it be?*

And this time, after ten days of silence, it was him.

MICHAEL: Hi. Would you like to go on a sailing trip with Megan and I Thursday afternoon? Just the three of us.

Cindy reread the message several times before Tracey yelped out, "Are you ever going to tell me what you're reading? I'm dying over here."

Cindy placed her phone in front of Tracey and watched as her sister scanned Michael's words.

"Is there any chance he wants to take me out to the Straits and drown me?"

Tracey rolled her eyes. "You and I both know that this is a good thing. He's had his deep 'Michael thinking time,' and he's come up with something to say."

"Yeah. He's decided to break up with me as a mother," Cindy returned.

"You have to give this kid a little more credit," Tracey scolded. "He's about to be a father. He probably has a lot more compassion for that sort of thing than you could even imagine."

* * *

The mother-daughter-son sailing expedition was slated to begin at twelve-thirty, two days later, on a gorgeous Thursday not long before the "official" start of summer. Already, Mackinac Island residents were tanned and bright-eyed with the optimism that the season allowed. Tourists buzzed in and out of

The Grind as Cindy passed by, holding paper cups of coffee and dropping their sunglasses across their noses. Cindy peeked a glance through the doorway to find Wayne and Michael in conversation behind the cash register. Michael was already dressed in an all-white sailing outfit, while Wayne wore his typical black button-down.

Cindy, who hadn't seen her son since that fateful day at the festival, exhaled all the air from her lungs and tried to drum up the courage to speak to him again. But before she could press into The Grind to greet Michael, a bright, "Mom! Wait up!" met her ears. She turned to find Megan in a bright yellow dress, skipping toward her.

"You've been such a hermit," Megan said tenderly as she threw her arms around Cindy. "I've been worried about you."

Cindy burrowed her chin into her daughter's shoulder and inhaled the strawberry scent of her hair. When she stepped back, she could see the truth reflected in Megan's eyes.

Megan knew the truth. And probably, based on what Cindy had shared down in East Lansing, she'd put two and two together and realized that Jeremy was the true father of Michael.

"This is going to be hard for me," Cindy whispered, her voice wavering.

"You can do it," Megan told her. "I believe in you."

The bell over The Grind's door jangled as Michael stepped out. His face was open yet unsmiling, and he carried a little cardboard container in which he'd propped up three coffees.

"I made you a cappuccino, Mom," he told her timidly. "I know how much you like them."

"Thank you." The milky, foamy coffee traced down her tongue as she sipped. As her heart skipped around in her chest, she forced herself to lift her eyes toward her son's. There wasn't anything to say, not there on Main Street as the tourists streamed past, the horses clopping across the cobblestones.

They headed to the dock, with Cindy and Megan walking about three feet behind Michael. Megan chatted amicably about a few books she'd decided to read prior to her semester at Michigan State. Michael had read one of the books she'd decided on and told her what he'd appreciated about it, saying that he'd read it while driving through California, which had "really added to the experience."

"You've lived such a life, Bro," Megan said as Michael stepped onto Wayne's sailboat, *Tara*, and began to arrange the sails and the ropes. "Guess it's time to settle down, though. Become a dad..."

Michael's laugh was nourishing and alive, the way Jeremy's once had been. "I guess that's kind of the idea. It was a surprise, sure. But Margot and I have a good thing going."

Megan and Cindy arranged themselves on the boat as Michael raised the sails to catch the whipping winds just so. They rushed over the frothing waves, headed westward toward the Mackinac Island Bridge, and spits of water crested their cheeks and dampened their windbreakers. Cindy crossed and uncrossed her arms nervously, watching as her son worked dutifully to get them out to the other side of the island, where they could rest beneath the splendor of the sun.

"I brought snacks," Megan said playfully, unzipping her backpack to draw out a large box of cookies.

"And I brought some wine," Michael added, drawing out three plastic cups and a bottle of rosé, which suited the glorious near-summer-feel perfectly. He portioned out the wine and passed the glasses around as Cindy crunched at the outer edge of Megan's homemade cookies.

Maybe we'll never have to talk about it. Maybe we can just hang in the in-between of knowing and not knowing.

Megan dropped her head back to allow her gorgeous blonde curls to spill out across the edge of the boat. Michael perched off to the left, his tanned knees pressed against his chest. The tension of the silence was interrupted frequently by a cawing bird or the sudden and violent rush of the water beneath them.

Just say it. He deserves your honesty.

"Michael..." Cindy clutched her plastic cup with strong fingers; the plastic nearly gave way beneath them. "Michael, I don't even know where to start."

Michael glanced toward Megan, who gave him a nod of encouragement. Had Megan prepped Michael on what to do? Had Megan urged Michael to patch things up with Cindy? Maybe Cindy would never know.

"Maybe start at the beginning," Michael tried softly. "I want to know everything."

Cindy blinked back tears, took a long sip of wine, and forced herself to begin.

"Jeremy Miller was my best friend, my boyfriend, my partner, my everything. It was like we experienced the entire world as a team. Tara used to say that we were psychic, that we could have entire conversations across the table with one another without saying a word. For Tara, this was sometimes infuriating. She hadn't met Wayne yet and wondered if she would ever fall in love at all. But I digress..."

Cindy leafed through her purse to find the item she'd decided, last-minute, to bring along. It was a photograph of Cindy and Jeremy, taken weeks after their high school graduation at one of the bonfire parties on the other side of the island. In the photograph, Jeremy stood behind Cindy with his arms wrapped around her. He tilted his head as though he'd just whispered something unknowable into Cindy's ear. Cindy glistened with orange light from the sunset and wore a pair of jean shorts and a bikini top.

They looked like a picture-perfect American couple.

Michael accepted the photograph and stared down at this man, a man who, based on looks alone, could have been

Michael's brother. When his eyes rose to meet Cindy's, Cindy just nodded as her throat tightened.

This is your father.

After another full minute, Cindy drummed up the courage to tell him what had happened next. The accident, the pregnancy, and the fear of being a single mother. "I wanted us to blend easily as a single-family. I didn't want you to start off your life with all this pain. But it was almost like you sensed it anyway. Kids are intuitive. And Fred..."

"Always hated me," Michael finished. "It didn't take a genius to figure that out."

"I don't think he set out on his journey with me to be cruel to you, Michael," Cindy whispered, her voice cracking. "He always wanted to be a father. But after Megan... I learned that I couldn't have any more children. I think he resented that he was only allowed to have one child of his own. He eventually resented me, which extended to you. I am so sorry, Michael. By then, I couldn't imagine splitting up our family."

Michael and Megan exchanged glances, both with similar characteristics that played out over their cheeks and lips. These, Cindy knew, were Swartz features; she'd brought them into their world.

The three of them fell silent for the better part of the next half-hour as Michael whipped the sailboat further out along the Straits of Mackinac. Bit-by-bit, Cindy's shoulders loosened; her heart lifted into her throat. She felt strangely light as air, as though she'd finally allowed the burden of her past to sink to the bottom of the lake.

When they finally tied up the boat for the afternoon back at the Mackinac Island docks, Michael and Cindy hugged silently yet powerfully, both overwhelmed with the nature of their relationship. Michael gave her a nod and finally whispered, "I have a lot to think about." He then stepped off the dock and bounded back toward the home he shared with Margot, the home where, very soon, he would become a father.

Cindy buzzed her lips distractedly, fearful that he'd decide he didn't want her in his life after all. Megan slid her fingers through Cindy's and tugged her down the dock.

"That went better than you think it did," Megan told Cindy firmly, with the authority of a woman who would one day achieve all her dreams. "You just have to give him time."

When Cindy returned to Tracey's house that evening, she found a letter in the mailbox. On the envelope, Fred's handwriting had scrawled: **CINDY**.

Cindy was reminded of birthday cards and little notes across her kitchen that said: NEED PAPER TOWELS and MEGAN AT SOCCER.

She was reminded of a very long life she'd lived with this man by her side.

Her hands shaking, she opened the envelope and slid out a paper he'd torn out of a notebook that they kept on the counter.

CINDY,

Maybe we'll never fully understand each other.

I'm done trying.

Find in this envelope divorce papers that have been drawn up by my divorce lawyer in St. Ignace.

In the meantime, I've accepted a position at a skin care clinic in Detroit.

The house is paid in full, and it's yours.

Chapter Twenty-One

Cindy couldn't bring herself to return to the house at Pontiac Trail Head for another three days after receiving Fred's letter. To her, the house was basically haunted with memories, filled with ghost-like laughter from her time with Tara, the sound of Fred's sports television, or the giggles of her young children down the hall. When she finally did force herself to head up to the hill, leaf through her pockets for her keys, and push through the door, she half-expected a monster to emerge from the shadows and eat her alive.

But no. In truth, the house was just a house— and as she walked through the hallways alone, she sensed that the house was fully ready for its next stage.

That stage? It was all about Michael and Margot's coming baby.

To kickstart her new era in the big house on the hill, Cindy gathered the Swartz family for an impromptu baby shower. Everything had to be endlessly perfect: with barbecue chicken on the grill, salads with glistening vegetables and fruits, flowing wine, and little lemon, carrot, and ginger cakes with sweet and thick frosting.

Early on the morning of the baby shower, Megan, Emma, and Tracey arrived at Cindy's place early, burdened with the weight of party decoration supplies and more odds and ends from the grocery store. Megan dropped a large paper bag on the kitchen table and eyed the gleaming room, noting but not verbalizing the fact that Cindy had changed it already, a great deal. She'd removed the artwork that she and Fred had picked out and instead hung her own photographs along the walls, moments from both this year and the era in the nineties, right before everything had changed forever.

She'd even hung a tiny photograph of Jeremy, taken on a blissful summer's day the year before his death. She hadn't placed it in a prominent location; she'd just realized, with a funny jolt in her gut, that she'd spent too much of her life pretending that Jeremy had never existed at all. She was done with that.

"Is Ron coming this afternoon?" Tracey asked as she began to prepare a big pitcher of mimosas, a pre-baby shower treat for those who'd come to decorate.

"Actually, I asked him to pick up flowers," Cindy said with a laugh. "So, he'd better."

A few minutes later, there was a ding at the front door. Cindy leaped for the foyer and opened the door to discover Ron Waters himself, dressed in a light blue suit jacket and a pair of jeans. In his arms, he held what seemed to be twenty pounds of flowers— baby's breath and lilac and light pink roses. Cindy leaped forward to help him, gathering one-half of the flowers in her arms and very nearly brushing her lips against his cheek in the process.

"You should have gotten a cart!" Cindy said as she beckoned him into the house after her.

"I got a little carried away, and then I got cocky," Ron

admitted. "But you said they were important... And I had to listen to everything Bethany said about what flowers were best for a baby shower."

"She's been in this business longer than I've done anything in my life," Cindy affirmed. "She's to be listened to. That's for sure."

As Tracey, Emma, Megan, and Cindy flung themselves through the early afternoon's "decorating committee," Ron removed his suit jacket, borrowed a large t-shirt and a pair of ratty pants, and mowed the backyard. Cindy's heart swelled with emotion as she watched him pushing the mower from one end of the yard to the other.

"It's nice to have someone watching out for you," Tracey murmured as she walked past Cindy, her mimosa lifted. "No matter what happens between you, I have a hunch he'll have your back."

By three-thirty, Ron had showered and re-dressed in his suit jacket and jeans. He sat in the living room, surrounded by frilly baby shower decorations, and sipped a glass of wine. Tracey, Emma, and Megan sat on either side of him, chatting excitedly. A few minutes later, the doorbell rang to bring in Wayne and Elise, both carrying presents. Ron leaped up excitedly to chat with Wayne, who he'd apparently struck up a worthy friendship with. Elise joined the girls, beckoning for Penny to enter, as well. Cindy watched from the doorway as Penny, Megan, and Emma cozied up together, gossiping about some fresh twenty-something island drama.

When Dean arrived, his dog, Diesel, ambled toward the kitchen to place his nose directly on the table. He blinked at the cakes and the dips and the barbecue chicken longingly yet remained back a bit, knowing his place.

"Good boy," Dean muttered as he slid a hand along his dog's ears. "He can barely stand how good the food looks. Granted, neither can I."

"We have to wait for the guests of honor," Cindy told him warmly. "In the meantime, have I introduced you to my friend, Ron?"

Dean and Ron shook hands. Ron's eyes widened the slightest bit as though he was just as fearful as a teenage boy about to "meet the father" of a girl he fancied.

"Hello there!" Elise called joyously as the front door creaked open.

Cindy leaped for the foyer, her heart burning. She tore the door open the rest of the way to reveal them— her handsome Michael, dressed in a suit, and his darling girlfriend, the very-pregnant Margot, who wore a glittering white frock with puffy sleeves. There in the doorway, Margot and Michael held hands and peered at Cindy nervously. They looked as beautiful as any picture, youthful and filled with promise.

Cindy stepped forward to wrap her arms around them, dropping her head against Michael's arm and rubbing her cheek against the fabric of his suit. After a long and loving pause, she finally mustered the strength to speak.

"Michael, your father would be so proud of the man you've become. He was kind, and he was loyal, and he already loved you to smithereens when you were just a tiny idea, hardly anything at all."

Michael pressed a hand over his mother's shoulder and shivered against her, lost to the emotion of learning to love a man he'd never been allowed to know.

"I love you, Mom," Michael whispered finally. "Thank you for giving me this gift of the truth."

Inside, the Swartz family ambled forward, calling out greetings for the gorgeous couple. Clenching her eyes closed, Cindy stepped back to allow them to enter their party. Already, Margot was exuberantly complimenting the cakes, and the flowers with her hand stretched protectively over her stomach. For a moment, Cindy remained in the foyer, allowing the cool breeze off the Straits of Mackinac to flow across her cheeks, through her hair.

If only you were here to see this, Jeremy.

When she turned to close the door, her eyes locked with Ron's across the sea of family members. He gave her a nod of approval and a secretive smile.

Your story isn't done yet, she thought then. There's still so much to live for.

Other Books by Katie

The Vineyard Sunset Series

Secrets of Mackinac Island Series

Sisters of Edgartown Series

A Katama Bay Series

A Mount Desert Island Series

Connect with Katie Winters

BookBub
Amazon
Facebook
Newsletter

To receive exclusive updates from Katie Winters please sign up to be on her Newsletter!
CLICK HERE TO SUBSCRIBE